MW00936908

THE HOMECOMING

THE POTTER'S HOUSE BOOKS - BOOK 1

JULIETTE DUNCAN

COPYRIGHT

Cover Design by T.K. Chapin

Copyright © 2018 Juliette Duncan

All rights reserved

The Homecoming is a work of fiction. Names, characters, and incidents are all products of the author's imagination or are used for fictional purposes. Any mentioned brand names, places, and trade marks remain the property of their respective owners, bear no association with the author, and are used for fictional purposes only.

THE HOLY BIBLE, NEW INTERNATIONAL VERSION®, NIV® Copyright © 1973, 1978, 1984, 2011 by Biblica, Inc.™ Used by permission. All rights reserved worldwide.

I

PRAISE FOR "THE HOMECOMING"

Juliette continues to give us her readers, a very well written book that always points to God's grace and Love for His people. This book was a story of second chances...There are real life issues that are dealt with in a way that honors God and points the reader to the truth about God's character. *Margaret L*

Juliette Duncan's The Homecoming is a story of real life situations and being influenced through doubt turned into a strong faith in God. It shows it's never too late to accept Christ into one's life and be forgiven. Her stories are refreshing reads to counteract the violence and heartache that we experience daily through media or personally. *Jana*

This is a heart rending story about faith & forgiveness. A story about God's great love & forgiveness. Also a story about our judgmental attitudes...God does do amazing things when we have faith & trust in Him & don't give up on our loved ones not just in this story but in our immediate lives! *Patricia*

A NOTE FROM THE AUTHOR

The 21 books that form **The Potter's House Books** series are linked by the theme of *Hope, Redemption, and Second Chances.* They are all stand-alone books and can be read in any order. Books will become progressively available from March 27, 2018

- Book 1: The Homecoming, by Juliette Duncan
- Book 2: When it Rains, T.K. Chapin
- Book 3: Heart Unbroken, by Alexa Verde
- Book 4: Long Way Home, by Brenda S Anderson
- Book 5: Promises Renewed, By Mary Manners
- Book 6: A Vow Redeemed, by Kristen M. Fraser
- Book 7: Restoring Faith, by Marion Ueckermann
- Book 8: Unchained, by Juliette Duncan
- Books 9– 21 to be advised

Visit www.pottershousebooks.com for details of the latest releases updates.

ALSO BY JULIETTE DUNCAN

Contemporary Christian Romance

The Shadows Trilogy

Lingering Shadows

Facing the Shadows

Beyond the Shadows

Secrets and Sacrifice

A Highland Christmas

The True Love Series

Tender Love

Tested Love

Tormented Love

Triumphant Love

True Love at Christmas

Promises of Love

Precious Love Series

Forever Cherished

Forever Faithful

Forever His - coming soon

Middle Grade Christian Fiction

The Madeleine Richards Series

1

KAYLA

LIFE. *"But she who is self-indulgent is dead even while she lives."*

ADRENALIN COURSED through my veins as music boomed through the massive speakers into the packed arena thronging with adoring fans waiting for me to appear on stage.

Behind the curtain, I sucked in three deeps breaths. Then, with a nod to my manager, I pushed through the curtain, skidding across the stage to wild cheers and screams. "Thank you. Thank you all!" More screams erupted as those in the front rows stretched their hands out, trying to reach me. I smiled at them all. "How are you today? Ready for some hard rock?" They grew wild again.

I began playing my guitar and a hush fell over the arena. For the next two hours I poured my heart out. I gave them everything I had, and then some. This was my life, and I loved it.

As I waved goodbye, the crowd erupted again and

demanded an encore. I gave them what they wanted. I could sing all night, but Lawrence would have words about that. I sang two songs and then blew kisses as I jogged off-stage.

"Great job." Lawrence, my manager of five years hugged me before I collapsed onto the sofa.

"Thanks." My chest still heaved. I closed my eyes and took some slow breaths.

"Why didn't you tell me about the new song?"

"Because you would have said no." I didn't open my eyes.

He laughed. "Well, they loved it."

"Thank you."

"We'll use it as a bonus track on your new album."

I groaned. This was so typical of Lawrence, but I was too tired to discuss the contents of my new album with him right now. My adrenalin was wearing off and I needed a drink. I swung my legs off the sofa and headed to the fridge.

He followed me step for step like a devoted puppy. "Have you looked at the scripts yet?"

"Give me a break!" I rubbed my temple with one hand while holding the fridge door open with the other. The air was refreshing as I pondered the options. Wine, beer, water, flavored milk.

"You need to look at them. Opportunities like this don't come along every day. Given your current ratings, any show you choose would have you climbing the ladder to stardom."

"Stop it! I don't even know if I want to act." I chose a pint of strawberry milk and took a slug straight from the carton.

"You need to spread your wings, Kayla; don't put all your eggs in one basket."

I ignored his clichés and took another mouthful as I hitched myself onto a stool. All around, stage hands buzzed as they worked to tidy up after the concert. Two more performances and we'd be moving onto the next city. I couldn't even remember what city that was. Lawrence looked after all that. I just wrote the songs and performed. I took out my phone and flicked through my notifications. Three voice messages. I smiled at the first one. It was from Gregor, my latest boyfriend.

Ma chérie, you must be finished by now. Sorry I missed your show—I promise to be there before you wake tomorrow. Je t'aime. A tingle ran through my body as I imagined his soft voice purring in my ear.

I took another sip of milk, intentionally ignoring Lawrence as I listened to the second message, which was from my mom.

Hello sweetheart, it's Mom. Please call me; I haven't heard from you in a while and I miss you. We all do.

I sighed. My family lived in Shelton, a small conservative town in West Virginia no one had ever heard of. I often referred to it as *Sheltered*. I rarely went home to visit. My family, my mom in particular, didn't approve of my chosen lifestyle. She never had, and I doubted she ever would. I was the black sheep of the family. I didn't believe in their God, and I sang music they called songs of the devil. I'd given up trying to build bridges. I didn't care. Who needed a family, especially one that didn't support you? I had my family. My fans, my manager, my boyfriend. That was all the family I needed.

But as I listened to the third message, which was also from my mom, my insides cringed. This time she sounded angry. Disappointed. Shocked.

Kayla, what do you think you're doing dating a married man? What has become of you? You're breaking my heart. Mine and your father's. Please call!

"Your mother reads tabloids now?" Lawrence said, looking amused.

I shot him daggers that said *shut it*. He did. I rubbed my temples again. I was surprised it had taken three weeks for Mom to hear about my relationship with Gregor DuBois, the French actor I'd met at the Grammys and had instantly fallen in love with. Mrs. Steward, Shelton's self-appointed conveyor of gossip, had fallen down. Maybe she was ill. It had been all over the gossip magazines for weeks. *Kayla Mac and Gregor DuBois.* Just another Hollywood scandal. No big deal. So what if he was married? He'd left his wife months ago. Trust my mother to cast judgment yet again.

I needed something stronger than sweet milk. I walked back to the fridge and grabbed a bottle of wine and two beers. Turning, I almost bumped into Lawrence, who, despite my warnings, was still following my every step.

"Can you leave me alone?"

"You're not going to let it get to you, are you? You said yourself that your mother's a religious psycho."

"I've never said that." I never had. I might have thought it, but I'd never said it. But her message had ruined my night. I don't know why I let her get to me. I knew what she was like, but she was still my mother, and I her daughter. Why couldn't she be happy for me once in her life? I took a swig of wine and headed to my dressing room. Lawrence followed. I slammed the door in his face. He got the message and left me alone, but not before reminding me to tell him when I wanted to return to the hotel.

Really?

2

DANE

HOPE. *"For I know the plans I have for you."*

I SMILED and thanked God silently for each of the teenage boys He'd given me to nurture as they strolled into the meeting room that afternoon. Most of the boys chatted amongst themselves and returned my friendly greeting, but Ivan, the newest member of the group, barely raised his head. His baseball cap was turned backwards, not unusual for boys his age, but the way he wore it, with his long, blond hair poking out from under it, and his sullen expression, suggested he could easily rebel. I determined to get alongside him and prayed I could earn his respect and trust.

After tossing their school bags in one corner of the moderate-sized room, the boys made a bee-line for the serving counter where trays of mini bagel sandwiches, prepared lovingly by a group of ladies from church, freshly cooked popcorn, apple slices and chocolate brownies sat waiting for them. It didn't seem to matter how much food we had for these growing boys, they ate it all, even the apple slices, although they were always the last to go. I laughed as they stuffed their mouths. It didn't seem that long since I was their age, doing exactly the same thing in this very room. If only I'd heeded the advice of the group leader back then, but I was like Ivan, withdrawn, quiet, rebellious. God had had His work cut out with me, but He didn't give up on me. But if I could help Ivan avoid the same mistakes I'd made, I'd be a happy man.

"Like a game of ping-pong?" I asked as he took a mouthful of pop. He stood on his own, and I was a little annoyed with the other boys who seemed to be ignoring him. I'd have to have words with them, but at least it gave me the chance to get alongside him.

He shrugged as if he didn't care. I handed him a paddle. He took it.

Hitting the ball back and forth afforded little opportunity to chat, and he didn't seem interested. Or skillful. After he lost each game, even after I tried my best to let him win, I suggested we sit in the bean bags at the end of the room and listen to music. The other boys were playing pool or half-court basketball. Ivan didn't seem interested in doing either. In fact, he didn't seem interested in anything.

"What music do you like?" I asked as he followed me to the other end of the room. I already guessed his music of choice wouldn't be what we had available, given we were in a church building in a conservative Appalachian town where anything other than hymns and worship music was considered evil. I'd been trying to convince the older folks that not all modern music was bad, but it was an uphill battle.

He shrugged again, his hands shoving deeper into the pockets of his faded blue jeans.

"You must have some favorites."

"The usual. Ed Sheeran, Bruno Mars, Kayla Mac." He finally spoke, and I was grateful, but mention of Kayla knocked me off balance. It shouldn't have. Although born and bred in Shelton, her fame and success in the pop industry was looked down on by the town folks. She'd gone the way of the world, and very few parents allowed their children to listen to her music. Ivan's parents mustn't have cared. Which made me wonder why he'd come to Boys' Club in the first place.

"Sorry, I don't have any of their music. But I do have some cool guitar tracks." I selected the album I thought would be the closest to what he'd like, and pressed play. "Take a seat."

He sat.

"So, what brings you to the group?" There was no harm in asking, but somehow I didn't expect an honest answer.

"Mom said I had to come."

That was honest. I'd guessed as much. Parents often sent their boys to the group hoping I could miraculously fix them. Only God could do that, but I did my best to be His hands and feet with these kids. I was blessed to have this role, and I'd seen many a mixed-up kid grow into a mature man of God, and it warmed my heart. I prayed Ivan would be one of those, but I sensed it would take time. It didn't matter. God was in the business of changing peoples' hearts, gently shaping them to become what He intended them to be. And I had the privilege of seeing Him at work.

"That's okay. I'm glad you've come." And I was. Ivan might be sullen and rebellious and difficult to talk with, but he was just a kid needing love and acceptance.

We chatted for a while. Well, I chatted. Ivan grunted and shrugged, offering an occasional one-word answer here and there. It was a start.

At half-past four, the other boys strolled in and joined us on the bean bags. They knew the drill; it was talk-time. I straightened and grabbed my well-worn Bible from the shelf beside me, and as I did, I prayed that God would lead me in this special time.

"Hey guys, let's open in prayer."

All apart from Ivan bowed their heads. It didn't worry me. God would hear even with eyes open and head raised. It didn't matter to Him, but I guess bowing one's head was an act of humility and respect. I bowed mine as well.

"Dear Lord, thank You for being here with us this afternoon. Thank You for loving each and every one of us, and for being interested in all we do. Please help us grow closer to You and to learn Your ways so we can live our lives in a way that is pleasing to You. Amen."

A round of *Amens* followed. I drew a deep breath, opened my Bible to Proverbs 4, verse 23, and read it aloud. *"Above all else, guard your heart, for everything you do flows from it."*

The group's focus had always been on how to live for Jesus in a world that shunned His ways. It was hard, especially when young, and temptations abounded. Did I know about temptation! Today I'd decided to share my testimony with the group. They'd heard snippets before, but I felt the Lord leading me to share it more fully with them. Maybe it would help them open up, because this group in particular seemed reluctant to share their true struggles. They said the right words, but that wouldn't help when temptation faced them, as no doubt it would.

"I wish I'd taken that verse to heart when I was your age. I might not have a troublesome leg if I had." I rubbed the offending limb and sighed. I could never compare myself to the great Paul, but I too had been given a thorn in the flesh. It kept me humble and reminded me often of the consequences of sin. It also kept my focus on Jesus as I trusted Him for my daily needs. I wasn't a cripple, but sometimes I felt like one. I prayed that one day God would heal my leg completely, but in the meantime, it was my cross to bear. I'd learned a lot in my twenty-seven years. I prayed these boys could learn from my mistakes and not repeat them.

I began my story. "As a child, I was quiet and shy. I gave my life to Jesus at age ten, but I'd lived a sheltered life, and so when I joined the Marines at the age of eighteen, *the real world*, as I soon came to call it, I forgot the things I'd learned and took to drinking and partying with my newly-found friends. I also discovered I had a temper when intoxicated and landed myself in fight after fight. It was after one of those fights that I had my accident.

"Will was my friend, but you'd never know it that day. I couldn't even remember why we were fighting, only that we were. I was angry about something and I lost control and punched him. He punched me back, and then we traded punch for punch until the other guys stepped in and separated us. We'd be in trouble; fighting was strictly forbidden, and as a result, my mind wasn't on the job when the accident happened. It was an engineering *miscalculation* on one of the planes being tested during training. A miscalculation caused by my distracted body and mind. The small plane toppled, crushing my leg. Amputation was considered, but thankfully the surgeon managed to save it. Now my leg was held together with metal.

"I came home with my body and pride wounded. My family and church welcomed me home as if I were a war hero. I hadn't even made it out of training. God worked on my heart and gently brought me back to Himself, but not before years of depression, bitterness and regret. I even tried to take my life."

I sighed. Recalling the despair of that time brought it all back; it had been like walking through the valley of the shadow of death, only I was alive. I continued with my story. "But praise God, He turned my heart around after my suicide attempt. I came to accept that the injury was a direct consequence of my disobedience, of not guarding my heart, and one that I might have to live with every day of my life, but that was nothing to losing my soul. God would give me strength to live with my disability and would use my story to help others."

The boys stared at me. Maybe I'd said too much. I rarely spoke about my suicide attempt, and these boys, who were also living a sheltered life, had most likely never heard anyone talk about such things before. But if they weren't prepared to handle the real world, they too could make mistakes like I had. Hearing my story now might stop them doing something similar one day in the future.

"How *do* we guard our hearts?" I looked around at the boys, giving them time to think. It was a rhetorical question; I didn't expect them to answer. "You've probably heard the saying, *Sow a thought, reap a deed. Sow a deed, reap a habit. Sow a habit, reap a character. Sow a character, reap a destiny.*" Some of them nodded. I smiled. "Everything starts with what we think about, what we put our focus on. Before we do anything, we think it, whether we realize it or not. Thoughts lead to attitudes; attitudes lead to actions. Everything begins with the thought life. Our actions and achievements are the sum total of our thoughts."

I could see a lot of puzzled faces. It wasn't an easy thing to understand, but it was so important.

"So, how do we control our thoughts?" Once again, I didn't expect an answer. I didn't get one.

"By being careful about what goes into our minds. It's important to only think pure thoughts. Did you know that God made us such that we can only have one thought at a time in our minds?"

They shook their heads.

"It's true. Think about it." I let out a small laugh before becoming serious again. "So how do we keep from thinking wrong thoughts?" I paused. No one answered.

"Okay, it's quite simple. Just choose to think about what's right. If you're thinking about what's right, you can't think about what's wrong."

By the blank looks on their faces, I realized this had gone over their heads. If only I had the words to reach them and make them understand. But I wouldn't worry. God would do the work in their hearts, not me. It was my job to plant the seed. "We'll leave it there for today unless anyone has any questions." I looked around at the group. Ivan's head was lowered and I couldn't see his face. I had a sinking feeling he'd stopped listening at my first word.

Chad, one of the boys I could always rely on to ask a question, raised his hand. "So what do you do when all your friends are talking about bad things? How do you stop yourself thinking the same?"

I smiled. At least one of them had been listening. "Great question, Chad. That kind of thing happens all the time. It's only through God's grace in our lives and by focusing our attention on Him that we can keep our thoughts pure and clean. It's a choice we have to make, and it's not easy, but if we truly want to live for God and experience all He has in store for us, it's one we'll make gladly. We'll explore this further next week, so unless anyone else has another question, let's close in prayer."

I waited a few seconds and then bowed my head. "Lord God, it's not easy being a Christian in a world that has walked away from You. In a world where anything often goes and it's hard to keep our thoughts, let alone our actions, pure. Help us to focus our thoughts on You, Lord God. Transform our minds and let us experience the abundant life You promise to all those who follow You. Bless these boys, dear Lord. Let them shine like beacons on a dark stormy sea. Give them strength to live for You. In Jesus' name. Amen."

A few of the boys wiped their eyes quickly and tried to pretend they hadn't been crying. I didn't say anything, but my soul was gladdened that God's Spirit had been working in their hearts despite my fumbling words.

A knock on the door made me look up. Tom, the church janitor, poked his head in.

"Sorry, I tried to give you more time, but it's getting dark."

"We're just finishing now, so it's all good."

The boys jumped up from the bean bags and began tidying up. I had them well trained. Ivan hung behind and offered to help me up. It was a kind gesture, and I accepted, even though I could manage.

"That was a good lesson."

I blinked. I hadn't expected him to say anything like that, especially so soon. "Thank you."

"Can I... can I come to your shop sometime?"

I blinked again. "Of course. Drop by anytime."

"Cool." With that, he turned and joined the other boys as they grabbed their bags, leaving me smiling. God was good.

ON MY WAY HOME, I stopped at the grocery store to grab a few things. I groaned when Mrs. Steward, a little old lady from church, waved at me from the other end of the aisle. I quickly asked for forgiveness. She meant well; she just had a habit of gossiping, and it was hard to get away from her when she started.

"Dane! How are you?" She hobbled towards me. There was no escape.

I smiled politely. "I'm great, thanks. How are you, Mrs. Steward?"

Her expression grew somber. "I'm fine, but it's so sad about Mr. McCormack. Have you heard?"

My ears pricked up at the mention of Kayla's father. The McCormacks were members of our church, and although Kayla was rarely talked about, being near them made me feel close to her. Not that she ever remembered who I was. Any time she was in town and saw me, she looked right through me as if I didn't exist. I guess to her I didn't. "No, I haven't heard anything. What's wrong?" I didn't want to partake in gossip, but this sounded serious.

"They think he has cancer."

My eyes widened. *Cancer? Mr. McCormack?*

"And to receive such news when they're already going through such a difficult time with that daughter of theirs."

I'd heard about Kayla's latest scandal and didn't want to discuss it. Especially with Mrs. Steward.

I opened my mouth to say how sorry I was to hear about Mr. McCormack, but I was too slow.

"She's involved with a married man. Of all things, to shame her parents like that. They're such good people. I wonder what happened to that poor girl?" She leaned in closer. "It's the music lifestyle, I tell you. They're a rotten lot, all of them. Walking around with their skin covered in ink as if they're paintings. Singing the devil's music. It's disgraceful."

I drew a deep breath. "It's not our place to judge, Mrs. Steward. We're all sinners before God, just some of us are saved by His mercy and grace. We don't know what's going on in Kayla's heart, only God does."

She frowned and looked a little flustered. "Well yes, I guess you're right. I must get on. Nice talking with you, Dane." She nodded her head and scurried away as fast as she could.

I chuckled. "And you, Mrs. Steward," I called to her back. I hoped I hadn't sounded too pompous, but it was the truth. It wasn't our place to cast judgment. Kayla's lifestyle choices might be questionable and we might not approve, but we still needed to show her love. God did, even though His heart might be breaking, as no doubt her parents' hearts were.

But it seemed they now had something else to concern them. *Cancer?* My heart went out to them and I sent up a quick prayer as I finished my shopping.

3

KAYLA

DESPERATION. *There is no fear in love, but perfect love casts out fear.*

"OH, *ma chérie*. You've been crying."

I opened my eyes and gazed into eyes of magnetic blue. At forty-four, Gregor was eighteen years my senior, although you'd never know it. His youthful, sensuous appearance had earned him many an acting role in romance movies and television serials, and women all over the world would give anything to be in my shoes.

He brushed my cheeks gently as I stretched and threw my arms around his neck. He began kissing me, his mouth covering mine hungrily. I wanted to respond, but I couldn't ignore the banging in my head. I reluctantly pushed him away.

"I'm sorry, Gregor. I've got a hangover."

"*Pauvre bébé.* What can I get you?"

I blinked my eyes and put my hands to my head to stop it spinning. "Water, coffee, and drugs."

"In that order?"

"Yes." I covered my mouth and darted for the bathroom, reaching it just as the entire contents of my stomach emptied into the toilet bowl. I slowly dragged myself to the basin and splashed my face, wincing at my reflection; I looked like death warmed up. From my research, I knew Gregor liked his women to look good at all times. It was the last thing I felt like doing, but to keep him happy, I'd make the effort.

I pulled out my cosmetic bag and started work. Within minutes, my face was transformed to what I hoped would gain his approval. I slipped on my lip ring before leaning in to study my teeth, concerned that the whitening treatment was starting to wear off. It wasn't. My teeth were as white as pearls.

"Coffee's ready, *ma chérie*." I'd never tire of hearing Gregor speak to me like that. He overdid it for sure, but I didn't mind. For once, I had a boyfriend who not only said he loved me but truly did.

"Coming." I stole one last glance in the mirror, threw on my robe to cover my skimpy silk pajamas, and then opened the door.

"Ah, beautiful." Gregor's gaze caressed my body as it traveled from my bare feet to the top of my blue-black hair. Shivers of delight ran through me. I almost forgot my pounding head.

I side-stepped him teasingly and popped the pills on the counter into my mouth, washing them down with a glass of water. Picking up my coffee, I eased onto the plush leather sofa, placing my feet on the footrest and leaning back against the soft Italian leather. Gregor slid in beside me and nuzzled my neck.

"You should take a break, *ma chérie*. The tour is wearing you out."

I was reluctant to tell him the real reason I'd overindulged. Better that he think it was the tour taking its toll than my mother's opinion of our relationship. "I can't, you know that."

"Come to Paris with me. I don't want us to live like this." He nibbled my ear.

I sipped my coffee and tried to ignore the thudding of my heart as Gregor's warm lips grazed my neck. He'd been wanting me to take a break from my tours and performances since the day we'd started dating. I guessed it was so I could be by his side in *his* career, but what he didn't understand was that I wouldn't give up mine for anything, even him. We were at a stalemate. "I don't want us to live like this either, but I can't leave the tour right now. Maybe later."

He straightened, and I could tell he was pouting. For a mature man, he acted quite childish sometimes. "If you won't come with me, I guess we're over."

I almost spilled my coffee as I jerked up. He wasn't serious, surely. But how dare he make an ultimatum like that! "I can't give up everything I've worked for, Gregor. You know that. Can't we work something out?" I stroked his arm, desperately wanting him to change his mind. "I thought we had something special."

"We do, but not if we're oceans apart."

He had a point, but he could stay in America. He had movie offer upon movie offer. He didn't have to return to Paris, so why did he expect me to give up everything? "Why don't you stay here?"

He laughed. "I was only teasing. I like seeing how far you'd go for me. Of course I'm staying."

It was my turn to pout. I hated the way he thought he had me wrapped around his little finger, as if I was his puppet. Maybe I was, even though I baulked at giving up my career for him. Despite my annoyance, I was glad he was only teasing. I couldn't lose him. I'd lost too many boyfriends. I didn't want Gregor DuBois to be another statistic, even if my mother would never approve of him.

Words my mother had spoken to me years earlier flashed through my mind. *What does it profit a man if he gains the world, but loses his soul?* I pushed the words away. I didn't want to hear them. I hadn't lost anything, this is what I wanted, and nothing would make me change my mind. Not even the thought of losing my soul. I loved my life. I loved my fans. I loved Gregor DuBois.

I put my mug down and leaned my head against the corded muscles of his chest. "I'm sorry I pouted. *Je t'aime.*"

He pulled me close and kissed the top of my head. "You're forgiven, *ma chérie.*"

That was all I needed to hear. I was forgiven, and I was loved.

Gregor stayed until it was time to prepare for that night's concert. He promised to be there in the front row, but he never showed. A last-minute situation came up, so he said. I said it was okay, and I tried to convince myself it was.

Weeks passed. Gregor came to one concert, and even then he was late. I was clinging to him like a spider to a thread. Only this thread wasn't as strong.

That night, after the concert, as he began having his way with me, my phone buzzed. I knew who it'd be. My mother had been calling all afternoon, and I'd been ignoring her, assuming she'd be calling to plead with me to end my relationship with Gregor. I'd already told her she was wasting her time.

"Shouldn't you get that? It's the third time it's rung in as many minutes."

I sighed and pulled away. "It'll just be my mother."

"Mothers are important, *ma chérie*. Take it."

I said hello and froze as I listened to the words rush from her mouth. I'd prepared for a lecture; never in my wildest dreams was I prepared to hear that my father might have cancer. "We don't know for sure, Kayla. They're still doing tests, but we'd love you to come home. Please."

"Of course, Mom. I'll come right away."

When I ended the call, Gregor's brows were pinched.

"My dad has cancer…" I tried to keep my voice steady and my tears at bay.

"Oh. *Ma chérie*." He brushed his hand against my cheek before gathering me in his arms.

I sobbed into his shoulder as shock took hold. My strong, invincible, father, *dying?* It couldn't be; there had to be a mistake.

"Anything you need me to do, I'll do it," Gregor whispered into my ear.

"Thank you." It had to be a mistake. My dad wasn't sick, and the doctors would find that out sooner or later.

"Will you be okay? Would you like me to come with you?"

That would be my greatest joy. To take Gregor DuBois home to meet my family. To show them they were wrong about him, just like the doctors were wrong about my father's cancer. But that would never happen.

I straightened and wiped my face. "Thanks, but I need to go on my own." I forced a smile. "My dad's going to be okay, I just know it."

"I'll miss you."

"And I'll miss you. I need to pack."

"What about your tour?"

"I'll cancel it."

"Lawrence won't be happy."

"I don't care." And I didn't. For the first time in my life, I really didn't.

4

DANE

NEIGHBORS. *"In humility, value others above yourselves."*

THE FOLLOWING AFTERNOON I pulled up outside the McCormack's modest home on the other side of town. It surprised me that with all the money Kayla earned, she hadn't helped them move into a bigger home. But maybe they wouldn't accept money from her. I guess that wouldn't surprise me, knowing what they thought of her chosen career.

The house was pleasant enough. Like most folks in town, Kayla's folks took pride in their garden. In the front bed bordering the house, delphiniums with soft pink and blue flowers towered over shorter, but equally showy, peonies. Rustic pots with overflowing, brightly colored annuals lined the old timber steps.

I climbed those steps and knocked softly on the door in case Mr. McCormack was asleep. My eyes widened when he opened it.

"Dane Carmichael! Always a pleasure to see you." Stephen McCormack extended his large hand and greeted me with a broad smile. His trademark smile. It was a wonderful trait to have, but I wondered how he could still smile like that with the cloud of cancer hanging over his head.

I shook his hand. His grip was strong. Thankfully, the years working my potter's wheel had also strengthened mine, and I was his equal in this regard. It almost compensated for my weak lower limb. "It's good to see, you, Mr. McCormack."

"Please, call me Stephen."

I smiled and handed him the box of chocolates I'd picked up at the store.

"Your favorite, Stephen!" Marianne McCormack poked her head over her husband's shoulder. "How thoughtful, Dane. You're so kind. Come in. Please."

She ushered me in around Stephen, almost as if he were invisible. I laughed. Looking at the two of them, it didn't seem as if anything was wrong. I guessed faith did that to a person, helping them not to worry about their present circumstances, regardless of how bleak the outlook. But why couldn't they treat their daughter like that?

Mrs. McCormack ushered me and her husband into the small living room then went to make tea. The room was old-fashioned. Two large, dark brown recliner chairs dominated the room, but the photos filling the walls caught my eye. I stood and studied them. Photos from all phases of their lives, from their wedding to their grandson's first moments, proudly displayed for all to see. My gaze was drawn to one particular member of the family. *Kayla.* Kayla at age ten in that horrid dress she'd worn at the school talent contest. I still remembered it, just as I remembered how taken I was with everything about her all those years ago. Kayla at her school graduation, age seventeen or thereabouts. I was in the same grade, not that she knew it. I was invisible to her. The lack of photos of her since then spoke volumes.

"I suppose you're here because you heard the news?" Stephen sidled up beside me and folded his arms, as he too studied the wall.

I nodded, trying to stop the grimace I felt growing on my face. "It must have been a shock."

"Yes, but it's not confirmed yet. We're trusting God. If He decides my time's up, well, who am I to argue?"

I blinked. I knew Stephen was a staunch believer, but I didn't think I could be so calm and accepting if I were in his shoes. "You'll get treatment, won't you?"

"We'll see. Come and sit down." He pointed me in the direction of the closest recliner. He sat in the other. "Tell me, how are your folks? I missed them last week at church."

I filled him in on my parents' misadventure with their four-year-old triplet grandsons, my sister's children. One of them, Timothy, had broken his arm after jumping off the bed on the morning before Sunday service and they rushed him to the hospital. My mother felt so bad about it, but my sister said it had no doubt been Timothy's fault; he was always testing the limits.

We chatted a few minutes longer before Mrs. McCormack brought in the tea. She too asked me about my parents and then asked when I was going to settle down.

Heat rose and moved from my neck to my face. Not because of the hot, sweet, lemon tea I was drinking, but because of the question. This matter concerned my mother as well. She constantly reminded me that it wasn't good for me to be alone. I usually made a joke and changed the subject, but it was a matter that concerned me too, although I didn't tell anyone other than God.

"Don't give him a hard time, love. I was older than Dane when we met. He's got plenty of time to find the right girl."

I breathed a sigh of relief and gave Stephen a grateful nod.

Mrs. McCormack smiled at her husband with such affection. I couldn't help but hope that one day I'd find someone special to share the kind of love they had, but to date, no one in town had caught my eye or my heart. Besides, it would take a special person to love me with my disability. I needed to be patient and trust God, and in the meantime concentrate my attention on the Boys' group and my work.

"I know that, sweetheart," she said. "But I'd love him to find the same happiness we've had."

Stephen chuckled and reached for her hand. "Don't get sentimental just because I'm sick."

I didn't know where to look. I felt I was intruding on an intimate moment.

She shook her head. "I'm not. I'm serious. I'm praying that God will bring someone special into Dane's life."

"I'm sure He will, in His time."

I stood to leave after I finished my tea; I didn't want to outstay my welcome.

When I reached the door, Mrs. McCormack gave me a hug. "Come back whenever you want for a visit, Dane. But be warned, Kayla's coming tomorrow."

I tried not to react, but how could I remain unaffected by that piece of news she'd just thrown at me without warning? I forced myself to keep a steady voice. "Thanks. I'll keep that in mind."

I bid them both goodbye, pleased that Stephen was happy and seemingly well and not on death's door like the town folk had been saying, but unnerved by the news that Kayla McCormack would be home tomorrow.

5

KAYLA

CHOICES. *"See to it that none of you has a sinful, unbelieving heart that turns away from the living God."*

COMING HOME, if I could call it that, felt exactly the way it always did—weird. I was desperate to see my dad, but dreaded being recognized. Almost as much as I dreaded facing my mother. No doubt she'd exert pressure on me again to give up both my career and my boyfriend without even asking me about either.

Last night at the hotel, I'd quickly changed my hair color to brown, hoping that might keep me under the radar. Gregor said he preferred me with my blue-black hair, and once again asked if he could come. Again I told him this was something I needed to do alone. He didn't understand, but I couldn't explain further.

Lawrence had organized a rental car for me to collect from the airport. When I showed my license, the guy at the desk seemed oblivious of my fame, so I was safe, at least for a while.

I had a thirty-minute drive to prepare myself. Thirty minutes was not long, and before I knew it or was ready, I was pulling into the driveway of my family home. In four years, nothing had changed. The garden still looked as immaculate and tidy as ever. I could never live here. My life was neither immaculate nor tidy. It was messy, noisy and out of control. The way I liked it. But I had to admit, the garden did look nice.

A knock on the window of the car startled me; I hadn't seen anyone come down the steps. My mother stood there in gardening clothes giving an awkward wave. I unlocked the door and stepped into her waiting arms.

"Oh sweetheart, I've missed you so much!" she exclaimed as she embraced me, squeezing me tightly.

At five feet four, I was short compared to my mom's five nine, so the hug really was that, a proper embrace. When I was younger, her embrace had always made me feel safe, but now I felt caged and wished she'd let me go. "Mom, I need to breathe." I eased myself from her arms, and when I looked into her eyes, I wasn't surprised to find tears.

She lifted her hand and stroked my cheek. "It's so good to see you, Kayla."

I didn't say it, but I wondered if it really was. If she really wanted to see me, why did she never visit me? Not once had she been to one of my concerts or come to L.A. to spend time with me. She always expected me to come home. *Whatever.* This visit was about my father, not her and me.

I stepped away and grabbed my suitcase from the trunk.

"Let me help."

"It's okay. I can manage."

She tutted. "Always the independent one."

I pursed my lips. I had to hand it to her—less than five minutes and she was already at me. I slammed the trunk and faced her. "I've come home to see Dad. I don't want lectures or judgments. Okay?"

She stepped back, her mouth falling open.

"I'm sorry, but I don't want any of that. If you want me to stay more than a day, treat me like you want me here." I surprised even myself by how forthright and controlled I was.

"I'm sorry you feel that way, sweetheart. I'll try not to say anything about your lifestyle or that… " Tears filled her eyes. She quickly dabbed them with her gardening apron. I knew what she was about to say.

"Boyfriend?"

She nodded, dabbing her eyes again.

"I'm happy to talk about him but not if you're going to judge me."

She sniffed and blew out a breath, avoiding my gaze. "Come inside and see your father."

"That's what I'm here for. How is he?" I tried to keep my voice steady. I dreaded finding out, but I needed to know.

"He's doing well. We'll get the results tomorrow."

"I think it's a mistake. I don't think he's got cancer."

"You don't know that, sweetheart."

I didn't, but I was desperately trying to convince myself I was right.

Before we reached the top of the stairs, Dad opened the door and stepped towards me with his arms open wide. "My girl is home! Look at you! You're a sight for sore eyes." He laughed and pulled me close, picking me up in a tight hug like I weighed nothing at all.

I didn't want him to let me go, but after he put me down, I took a quick moment to study him. He looked well for someone who might have cancer, brightening my hope that the doctors were indeed wrong.

"I've missed you so much. I'm glad you've come home."

"So am I." And in that moment, I was. I forgot that my tour was on hold, about my manager's annoyance, about my mother's opinion of Gregor. I was home with my dad, and that was all that mattered.

"Come inside and let's catch up."

I linked my arm in his and stepped inside the house I knew so well. Before we even got down the hall, my older brother came down the stairs, stopping halfway and leaning over the rail, letting his gaze drift over my diminutive body. "Look who it is. Kayla Mac. I don't believe it." Adam's sarcasm hit hard.

We'd been close once, before I decided to follow my dream. I didn't understand why I had to be judged for doing the exact same thing he'd done when he decided to move away to study business as a career. I supposed leaving to study was acceptable but leaving to become a star wasn't.

"Adam." I forced a smile. "I didn't know you were here."

"I'm happy to have both my children home, although I regret it's because of my health that you've come," my father said.

"I've always visited, even before you got sick," Adam said defensively as he came the rest of the way down the stairs.

I rolled my eyes. "We're not children, Adam. It's not a competition."

My father held up his hands, "There'll be none of that in this house. Let's sit down and catch up while having some of your mother's wonderful tea."

Nothing had changed. Mother's tea fixed everything, according to my father. Whenever we argued, he always offered tea. For my father's sake, I decided to be civil and ignore my brother's accusing looks. I didn't know what I'd done wrong. I honestly didn't. All I'd done was follow my dream and now I was a star. What was wrong with that? Why couldn't they be proud of me?

As we sat in the living room, I studied my father more closely. Despite his cheerful demeanor, I realized that my earlier assessment was wrong. His skin held a yellow tinge and his eyes suggested he might be in pain. He still looked physically strong, but he'd lost a little weight. Maybe they were right after all. My shoulders sagged.

He caught me looking at him and patted my hand. "Don't worry. I'm going to be fine."

"Really? That's not just hopeful God talk, is it?

"We're trusting in God, whatever the outcome, Kayla."

I released a slow breath. I knew they'd do that. If God was so trustworthy, why did He let Dad get sick in the first place?

"Don't start, sweetheart. Let's just enjoy our time together, please?"

I drummed my fingers on the arm of the sofa, eventually nodding. I was here for him and needed to control my thoughts and words. I couldn't help looking at the pictures all around me, most of them of my nephew. The nephew I had yet to meet. I couldn't regret my choices now, not after my family had made it clear that we couldn't have a good relationship while I pursued my career. If I couldn't have both, then I had to choose. My mother came in with a tray of tea and snacks and I pulled my eyes away from the photos of the little boy, my younger sister Jennifer's son, Toby. Would I last long enough this visit to meet him? It was doubtful. I might not even last the night if this start was any indication.

My mother set the tray on the table and held out her hands. "Let's pray."

I groaned. My parents had a habit of praying over any little meal. I bowed my head but tried to shut out my mother's voice. *As if God would listen.*

"Lord, we thank You for our family, for Kayla and Adam's return, and we entrust Stephen's health to You. Thank You for this meal before us. Amen."

For my father's sake I sat there for the next hour, but after that I needed some air. I stood and wrapped my arms around his shoulders. "I'm sorry, Dad, I need to go out for a while."

Adam rolled his eyes. My mother glared at me. Dad patted my hand. "Come back soon, sweetheart."

I smiled at him. "I will."

I ran down the steps, beeped the car and jumped in. I didn't just need air, I needed a cigarette. Or a drink.

I headed straight to the store where I knew I'd find both.

I SLIPPED MY SUNGLASSES ON, even though it was late in the day, hoping no one would recognize me. I pulled up outside the store and dipped my head as I walked inside but removed my glasses—I was probably more conspicuous with them on. Instead, I draped my hair across my cheeks and slipped on a cap.

I quickly selected a bottle of wine and then stood in front of the wall of cigarettes. There were less options than in the past, which didn't surprise me. In this conservative town, not many people smoked. I scanned the rows looking for my brand of choice. It wasn't there. I'd have to try something different. As I stood trying to make my decision, I felt someone stop behind me. Without thinking, I turned my head. A young man, who looked vaguely familiar, stood looking at me. On second glance, I dismissed that thought. I didn't know him.

"They're no good for you, you know." His voice was soft. Gentle. Not judgmental, even though the words could have been taken that way.

"I do know that," I replied.

"Kayla?" He angled his head, his deep blue eyes fixed on me.

I stiffened. This was bound to happen sooner or later. "Maybe," I said offhandedly. I was actually amazed he knew who I was. He didn't look like a fan. Not that I had many fans in this town.

He was tall, perhaps six one, six two, with a slim build. If I could guess his age, I'd put him at around my age or maybe a year older. He had a thick head of hair, slightly darker than mine at the present time. His plain T-shirt and jeans suggested he was a simple soul. There were a lot of them in this town. He seemed tongue-tied.

"You were offering me wisdom about not smoking?"

He recovered and nodded, pointing to the wall of cigarettes. "Don't become a slave to them."

"Why? Because they cause cancer?" I bit my lip. The guy didn't deserve that. I was just angry that my dad, who'd never looked at a cigarette in his life, let alone smoked one, was the one who most likely had cancer. It was unfair. I might as well just smoke—what difference did it make?

"Partly. But mainly because of the control they have when you're addicted to them."

He was right. All addictions controlled. But did I care?

He gave me a small smile and said he'd see me around. As he walked away, I noticed he had a slight limp. I shrugged and returned my attention to the wall of cigarettes. I'd probably never see him again, but his words rang in my head.

I sighed and walked to the checkout, choosing instead to buy two packets of marshmallows and some lollipops to go with my bottle of wine.

I drove to the lake and parked, but after taking a swig and scarfing down half a packet of sweets, I gave up and returned home. Being with my dad was the only reason I was in this backwater town; I may as well return to L.A. if I wasn't with him. I just had to survive my mother and brother.

6

___

DANE

DESPAIR. *"Why are you so far away when I groan for help?*
Every day I call to you, but you do not answer."

Two days later I was sitting at my potter's wheel, throwing a
new pot, when a familiar figure with long, blond hair poked
his head into my workshop. I smiled and waved Ivan in. "Great
to see you. Glad you've dropped by." I didn't ask why he wasn't
in school.

As he entered, his hands shoved into the pockets of what
looked to be the same pair of jeans he'd been wearing the other
day at Boy's Club, his gaze traveled around the workshop
where I spent most of my days.

He stopped in front of the wheel, seemingly entranced by
what I was doing. "Thought I'd come and see what you
did here."

I chuckled. "I make pots, bowls, plates, anything that can be
made out of clay."

"Can I have a go?"

"Have you ever used a wheel before?"

"No. I've never even seen one."

"It's not as easy as it looks, but I'm happy for you to try. Sit on the stool and watch awhile."

After he sat, I slowed the wheel and showed him how to gently pull the clay into the desired shape. "Don't worry if it gets messed up. You can always re-do it." I showed him what I meant as I knew he'd be feeling anxious. It had taken me years to perfect my craft; he couldn't expect to make a perfect pot in one attempt.

After watching awhile, I told Ivan to wet his hands and place them on the clay. "It's okay. Just keep working it. Pull up slowly with one hand and support the clay with the other. That's the way."

The muscles in his neck eased as he got the hang of it. "How long do you do this for?"

"As long as it takes." I chuckled to myself. I could easily give him a sermon on how like this piece of clay we both were. It was one of the reasons I loved my work so much. It always made me remember how patient God had been with me, and still was. I was a work in progress, and so was Ivan. I wouldn't preach to him today, but as he sat there, gently shaping the clay, I asked God to reach deep into his heart and shape him into the young man He wanted Ivan to be.

"Are your hands growing tired?"

He nodded.

"Like me to finish?"

"Yes please."

I smiled and took over. He'd done a great job for his first attempt, and I told him so.

"What do you do once it's finished?"

"See that shelf over there?" I nodded to the back wall which was filled with unfired pieces I'd been working on over the previous few days.

"You've made all of them?" He sounded incredulous.

"Yep. Keeps me out of mischief." I chuckled again.

"How do you get them all shiny and colored?"

"Once they've dried out sufficiently, I fire up the kiln. It's over there." Once again I nodded in its direction as my hands were still working the clay.

His gaze shifted to the large kiln I'd built several years ago.

"They go inside, and the intense heat finishes the drying process, hardening and strengthening them." I could give Ivan a sermon on how God often allows us to go through intense situations which serve to make us stronger, but I thought I'd save that for another day.

"And then what?"

I laughed. He really wanted to know. "I glaze them to make them waterproof and glossy. Sometimes I paint them, it just depends. They go back into the kiln for another firing to harden the glaze. And then they go on display in the shop."

"Do you sell a lot?"

"Enough." I finished working the pot and slowed the wheel down, easing the almost perfectly shaped pot off the wheel and onto a tray.

"Do you need a helper?"

I raised a brow. "Are you after a job?"

"If there's one available."

I didn't need an employee, and I actually preferred working alone. However, how could I turn him down? It would provide a chance to get close to him and give him the support and mentoring he seemed to want and possibly need. I knew very little about his family life, but I could tell he was struggling with something.

"Sure. I could do with some help. Especially with my mail orders. And I can teach you everything else along the way."

His face lit up. "Really?"

"Really. You can start now if you'd like." I had a stack of orders that needed filling. Ivan would come in handy, especially with carrying the boxes to the van. My troublesome leg made that part of my job a challenge.

As we filled the orders, I tried to get him to talk about himself. I started by asking what instruments he played. I knew he played the guitar, but that was all.

"I used to play drums, but we had to sell them."

"That's a pity. Sounds like you enjoyed them."

He nodded.

"Anything else?"

"No."

"You've still got a guitar?"

"Yes. I'd like a better one, but…" He bit his lip, almost as if he regretted saying as much as he had.

I decided not to pry. He'd open up when he was ready.

"Maybe you could bring your guitar to Boys' Club and play for us one day."

"I don't think you'd like my music."

"You might be right, but we'd like to hear you before we make that call."

"Okay. You might regret it."

The little bell over the door jangled. When I was in my workshop, it was the only way I knew when anyone entered my shop, but as we were in there filling orders, we both looked up at the same time.

"Oh my God-"

I ignored Ivan's use of God's name, although I cringed inside. He obviously wasn't aware that God didn't like His name being used in vain, but I wasn't about to make him feel I was judging him after we'd made such good progress in such short time. There would be time enough to chat about these things in the days ahead.

But to be honest, I felt the same way. I blinked twice as Kayla walked in. I'd never expected her to come to my little shop, especially since it was on the opposite side of town from her folks' house.

Ivan's eyes were round like saucers. I could understand how he felt. From what he'd told me the other day at Boys' Club, Kayla was one of his favorite artists. To have her step into my shop had to be a dream come true, although I'm sure her visit would be common knowledge around town if Mrs. Steward got wind she was here.

Kayla ran her gaze over the shelves of assorted pottery items I had on display, seemingly unaware that Ivan and I stood on the other side of the counter. I guess I was used to that. Even at school, she'd never taken any notice of me, and I doubted she'd remember our brief meeting at the store two nights ago.

An aura of sadness hung over her that touched my heart. I understood why. I'd heard the news that her father did have cancer and the prognosis wasn't great. It made me wonder why she was here and not with her family.

Ivan lowered the box he held in his arms onto the counter.

She looked around. A glimmer of recognition crossed her face as her gaze met mine.

"Oh. It's you. I didn't know you worked here."

"You know her?" Ivan tore his gaze away from her and stared at me.

"Not really. We bumped into each other the other night, that's all." I wasn't going to make her feel uncomfortable by saying we went to school together when she obviously didn't remember. I turned my attention back to her. "Kind of. I actually own the place. Can I help you with something?"

"I was looking for a gift of some kind. I heard there was a gift shop on the edge of town. I didn't realize it was all pottery."

"There are lots of different types. I can help you choose something if you like. Who would it be for?" I tried to put her at ease as she seemed a little uncomfortable.

Shrugging, she shook her head and started to leave. "It doesn't matter."

"Wait!"

She stopped and turned around, a puzzled expression on her face.

I'd even surprised myself. I had no idea what to say, but as I looked into her sad, troubled eyes, I knew. "I'm so sorry to hear about your dad. He doesn't deserve it. He's such a good man, but I know him. He's strong, and he'll fight." I wanted to say that he'd be trusting God all the way, but I sensed that wouldn't go down too well. I just wanted to encourage her and let her know I cared. Not that it would matter to her. She didn't even know who I was.

Tears flooded her eyes. I didn't know what to do, but I couldn't let her stand there weeping. As quickly as I could I offered a tissue from the box on the counter. I would have liked to put my arms around her and comfort her, but that would have been entirely inappropriate, so I refrained.

She sniffed and smiled at me. "Thank you. What did you say your name was?"

"Dane. Dane Carmichael. Can I get you a drink of water?"

She nodded.

"I'll get it," Ivan offered.

He darted into the workshop where I kept a small fridge and returned seconds later with a bottle of ice-cold water and handed it to her. He was star-struck, but she was a mess.

She thanked him and then began to leave again.

"Kayla, wait."

She turned around again and faced me.

Once again, I didn't know what to say. My heart pounded although I knew nothing could ever develop between us. She had a boyfriend, and she was way out of my league, but my heart went out to her as a child of God who was hurting. "Would you like to talk about it?"

I expected her to say no. Why would she want to talk about her father's illness with a stranger? She surprised me when tears flooded her eyes again and she nodded.

"I'll... I'll leave you to talk." Ivan tipped his cap to her and then looked at me. "Let me know when you'd like me to come back."

I smiled at him, but as he was about to leave through the back door, I told him to wait and spoke to Kayla. "Ivan's one of your biggest fans. Can you give him an autograph?"

Ivan froze on the spot.

"Sure." Her voice was much softer than it had been the other night. She pulled a piece of paper from her purse, and taking a pen from the counter, signed her name and handed it to him.

His face expanded into a broad grin. "Thank you, thank you so much." His gaze darted to the paper and back to her. "It was nice to meet you, Kayla Mac."

"And you, Ivan?" She angled her head.

"Ivan Donahue." His voice wavered.

I smiled. She'd made his day, even though she was struggling herself. I always knew there was more to Kayla than people said.

After he left, I offered her tea or coffee. I felt strange having her in my workshop. It would have felt strange having any woman in my workshop, but Kayla? My childhood crush? I had to pinch myself that she was really here, standing in front of me, as large as life. Well, not large, exactly. If there was a word to describe her, it was petite. She was wearing flats today, not the heels she'd had on the other night, and even though I wasn't hugely tall, I towered over her.

Although she'd been my crush, I didn't know her. The thing that had so captured me when we were kids at school was her zest for life and her determination to do what she loved the most. Sing. Other than that, I knew little about her, but I sensed God had brought her to my workshop for a reason. Just like He had Ivan. So much for being on my own.

She smiled and said she'd like coffee if that was all right. I said it was and proceeded to make it. I apologized that I didn't have a fancy machine. She said it was okay as she wandered around my workshop inspecting my wheel, my kiln, and my wall of greenware waiting to be fired.

"You don't remember me, do you?"

She turned around and studied me, her brows coming together as she stepped closer. "You look familiar."

"We went to the same school since kindergarten."

"That can't be. I would have remembered."

"It's okay. I'm not surprised. I wasn't exactly social at school, but I was the boy who tied your ribbons together in the third grade." I decided to give her a break and held out my hand. "Dane Carmichael."

Recognition dawned on her. "I remember now. You stared at me when I sang at the talent contest."

"Guilty as charged." I chuckled as I finished making the coffee and carried two hand-made mugs of the brew to the outdoor table where I often ate my lunch. I liked being outdoors for at least part of my day, and the view to the hills always reminded me that God wasn't just a potter who worked on people's hearts, He was also the Creator of the universe.

"You said you know my dad?" She took my lead and sat at the table.

"Yes. I go to the same church as your folks."

Her lips pursed. I'd obviously said the wrong thing.

"I'm sorry, I didn't mean to upset you."

She let out a heavy sigh. "It's not you. It's just the whole religious thing I don't get."

"It's okay. We don't have to talk about that unless you want to. What would you like to talk about?"

She leaned back in her chair and stared into the distance as she wrapped her soft, tiny hands around the rough coffee mug. I couldn't help thinking how fragile she appeared. And it wasn't just on the exterior. "I don't know. Maybe my dad." Her voice wavered and she sniffed.

I handed her one of the tissues I'd stuffed into my pocket in case more were needed. "How is he?"

"Pretending he's okay."

"Maybe he is."

"Not you too?"

"Sorry. I didn't think." I chastised myself for being so rash with my words. Of course, Kayla wouldn't understand how a person could be okay with a bad prognosis. She'd let go of her belief in God and the hope of eternal life, so her dad's prognosis would be concerning and upsetting. I didn't know what she believed now, but it didn't matter. She was living without hope, and that made me feel sad for her. "Is he going to have treatment?"

"I think so."

"Well, that's good. Do they think it will be successful?"

She shrugged. "They don't know." She let out a frustrated sigh. "I want him to come home with me so he can get the best treatment he can, but he said he's happy to stick with the treatment here."

"Shelton has a great hospital."

"It's tiny."

"Maybe, but tiny doesn't mean it's not good."

"I just want him to get better." Tears flowed down her cheeks.

Again I wanted to wrap my arms around her and comfort her, but instead, I placed my hand gently on her shoulder. "I know you do. It must be so hard to see him sick and not know what the future holds."

She nodded as she blew her nose. "And they seem so calm about it. I can't do calm."

I wanted to share with her why they were so calm, but I

knew her heart wasn't open. I prayed that God would use her father's illness to reach her, to remind her of things she'd learned as a child, and that He would use me in any way He saw fit. "We all handle things in different ways. It's okay to be upset and sad, but maybe your dad needs you to be strong as well. I'm sure he'll do whatever he can to beat it. I don't think he's wanting to leave you just yet."

She sipped her coffee. "You're probably right. I think it's all the trusting in God talk I can't handle. I don't understand why they think they can trust God if He didn't stop my dad from getting cancer in the first place."

I groaned inwardly. I'd heard this argument so often and I could preach ten sermons on the topic, but I knew that none of them would go down too well right now. "Maybe you need to let it go for now, and just be there for your dad. I think he'd appreciate that."

She released a slow breath. I could almost see her brain ticking over. I didn't know what else to say, but I knew Stephen McCormack loved his daughter and would want her there with him. "I'll try."

I smiled. I guessed how hard that was for her to say. "So, can I help you with that gift?"

"Are you trying to get rid of me?"

I laughed. "Of course not. You can stay as long as you want." And I meant it. I might not have known the young Kayla very well, but I was liking the grown Kayla very much. Not in a romantic way, although I couldn't deny that thought hadn't crossed my mind, but as a friend. There was a lot more to her than most people realized.

"Okay, you can help me with a gift, and can I come back another time?"

"Absolutely. You're welcome whenever. How long are you staying in town?"

"I don't know. I'd like to stay as long as I can for Dad, but my manager's putting pressure on me to go back. I had to put my tour on hold, and he's not happy."

"He mustn't have a heart."

She laughed. "You might be right. Anyway, show me the gifts."

"Come this way." I grabbed my leg, a small groan escaping my mouth as a stab of pain struck when I went to stand. I tried to cover it, but Kayla looked at me with concern.

"Are you all right? Can I help?"

"It's nothing, but thank you." The pain left as quickly as it came, and I stood on my own. I headed back to the workshop with Kayla beside me.

"What happened, if you don't mind my asking?"

"A training accident when I was in the Marines. It's no big deal." I shrugged, not wanting her to feel sorry for me.

"Don't you get mad about it sometimes? At how it happened in the first place? I don't think I could shrug it off so easily."

I smiled as I guided her back into the shop. I needed to be careful how much I said so I chose my words carefully. "You never know how strong you are until you overcome something. I guess I'd rather have a good leg, but God's taught me a lot by having a troublesome one."

She grew quiet. At least she didn't refute what I'd said. "Well, you're stronger than I could ever be."

"I think you're pretty strong. I could never get up on the stage like you do."

"Have you been to a concert?" Her face lit up.

I didn't want to disappoint her, but I couldn't lie. "No, but I'll never forget your first performance."

She laughed. "My concerts are a lot different now. Maybe you should come to one."

"Maybe I will." I needed to change the conversation before I got myself into trouble. I turned to the display shelves. "Let's find that gift."

We spent the next few minutes choosing something suitable. I didn't ask who it was for. I didn't want to know. She chose a fruit bowl that I'd spent many hours creating and decorating. I didn't tell her I knew every single detail of it, from the almost invisible indent on one side where I accidentally knocked the unfired bowl against another, to the tiny specks I'd added to the strawberries to make them look real. I knew exactly how many specks there were, just like God knew exactly how many hairs she had on her head. It was my precious creation and I was happy for her to have it. I refused to let her pay for it. "It's a present from me to you."

"You're so sweet, Dane. Thank you so much."

"You're welcome. And please come back whenever you want."

"I will. Thank you."

As I watched her walk to her car, I couldn't help but wonder if she would. Why would a star like Kayla want to come back and visit a potter with a troublesome leg? I shrugged. I guess I'd wait and see, and in the meantime, I'd pray for her and her family.

7

KAYLA

FAITH. *"Now faith is confidence in what we hope for and assurance about what we do not see."*

I'D SPENT the entire evening researching pancreatic cancer. I hadn't even known where the pancreas was before my dad was diagnosed, and what I read distressed me. My father had seemed invincible, but now the possibility that this cancer might be incurable was starting to sink in and I was devastated. I could lose him.

I needed to talk with somebody. Gregor, ideally, but despondency swept over me as I scrolled through his messages.

Apologies, ma chérie, I can't talk right now. I'll call soon. Je t'aime.

Sorry, sweetie. I got held up at my last shoot. Will call in the morning.

My phone's about to die. I'll call as soon as I can.

Two days later I was still waiting. I tried to convince myself everything was all right between us, but I had a sinking feeling it wasn't. But I missed him so much.

I needed a drink. I needed to forget about my dad's cancer, that he might die, about Gregor, about everything. Mom didn't allow alcohol in the house, but I had a stash in the car.

The house was quiet and dark as I stepped out of my room and tip-toed downstairs. A beam of light shone from the kitchen. I groaned. I didn't want to bump into anyone, especially my mother. But something told me it wasn't her. When I was a teenager, Dad and I often met in the kitchen for a late-night feast. He had trouble sleeping, and I liked being with him.

I poked my head around the corner and smiled. "Dad?"

He was face deep in a tub of ice cream and looked up guiltily.

I laughed. "Can I join you?"

He wiped his face and waved me in, holding a finger to his lips.

I grabbed a bowl and a packet of tiny marshmallows from the cupboard. He scooped some strawberry ice cream into my bowl, and as I sprinkled some marshmallows on top, I shook my head at him again in amusement. It felt like old times, with strawberry ice cream still our favorite as it had been back then.

"I've missed your laughter, Kayla."

I looked at Dad and sadness gripped my heart. It really had been years. I shouldn't have allowed the friction between my mother and me to stop me coming home. I could have made time; I didn't perform every night. It had been my choice. If only my mother could accept me for who I was, not what she wanted me to be.

"Are you afraid, Dad?"

"Of the cancer?"

I nodded. "And of maybe not getting better."

He set his spoon down and placed his big hand gently over mine. "I don't think so. But the thought of leaving you all does make me sad."

"I hope it doesn't come to that."

"I hope it doesn't either, sweetheart."

"It's so unfair."

"Death's a natural part of life."

"But you're too young to die." I looked deep into his eyes, willing him not to give up.

"I know you don't understand, but I'm trusting that God has this all under control. I don't want to die just yet, and your mother and I are hoping that the treatment will be successful, but God is bigger than all of this. We see things from our earthly perspective, which is so limited and small. God sees things differently. Our life here on earth is just a speck compared to eternity, and if I were to die before my time, I know where I'll be spending eternity, and I'm excited about that."

My brows pinched together. "Excited about dying! I don't know why you're so sure heaven exists." I searched my father's face. Out of everyone in this family, he was the only one who didn't exasperate me. I'd grown up with all of this religious stuff, but it seemed to me that it was just a fairy tale made up to help people feel better about dying. But my dad was sensible and down to earth, so if he believed it, maybe it could be real. I doubted he'd believe something just because he was supposed to.

He stroked the top of my hand. "Do you love me?"

I frowned. "Yes."

"Why do you love me?"

I frowned again, not sure how to answer that. I shrugged. "Because you're my dad."

He laughed. "It's that simple? You love me because I'm your dad?"

I nodded, waiting for him to explain.

"And how do you even know that I'm your dad?"

That was a good question, something I'd never thought about. *How did I know he was my father?* He'd just always been my dad. He'd always been there, caring for me, looking out for me. He was married to my mother. My forehead creased. *How did I know that Mom was actually my mother?* The same thing, I supposed.

Dad chuckled. "I can see you figuring that answer out."

"What's the point of it all?"

"The point is that I *am* your dad. You don't need any proof of it nor have you ever doubted it. You just had faith that it's true."

"Should I get a DNA test?" I laughed nervously.

"Would it change anything if you found out you were adopted?"

I thought about it for a second. It would certainly be a shock, but I'd never known any other dad. Dad was my dad, regardless of whether I was adopted or not. But I still needed to know. "Am I?"

"Of course not. Don't you remember when I spoke to you in your mother's tummy?" He winked.

I laughed. My dad would never change. "So what are you saying, oh wise one?"

"I'm saying, oh stubborn one, that I believe in God just like you believe that I'm your dad. I've never doubted, and no matter what the situation, He's still my Father. Even if He'd told me that I'd have a daughter who'd go off and do her own thing, I would still have chosen to have her ten times over."

"Dad..."

"I'm not trying to make you feel bad, I'm just trying to explain. If He said He had a place prepared for me, I have no reason not to believe Him. He wouldn't lie to me, just like I wouldn't lie to you. He's a good Father."

"If He's so good, why did He let you get sick in the first place."

"Like I said before, we see things differently than God. He could have stopped me from getting sick, but maybe He has a greater purpose that we're not aware of."

"Then why pray if He won't do anything about it?"

"Oh, Kayla. We don't know that He won't. He might see fit to heal me, or He might see that it's better for me to go home. Praying is really just talking to Him, you know that. I've told Him I'd like to hang around here a while longer, but I've also told Him that I'm prepared to leave the final decision to Him, because I know that the end of my life on earth is just the beginning of my life in eternity with Him. And because He's my Father, He only wants the best for me."

"You know I don't believe all of that." I let out a heavy sigh and shoved a spoonful of ice cream into my mouth. I'd heard it all before; so often, in fact, I used to tune out.

I returned to my room a little later without fetching that bottle of wine. I couldn't bring myself to get wasted after being with my dad; I'd already disappointed him enough for one lifetime.

8

DANE

CONTENTMENT. *"Godliness with contentment is great gain."*

ALTHOUGH I LIVED in a separate dwelling at the back of my parents' house, I often found myself in my mother's kitchen, partly because her cooking was better than mine, but also because I enjoyed her company.

"You seem lost in thought today, Dane." She glanced at me as she lifted a batch of cookies she was baking for my nephews from the oven. They smelled delicious, and I hoped she'd let me have at least one or two. She was right. I was lost in thought. I was a little pensive after having two unexpected visitors to my workshop the previous day.

I shrugged. "I'm okay."

"I didn't say you weren't!" She laughed. "Was that Kayla McCormack I saw coming out of the shop yesterday afternoon?"

I chuckled. My mom didn't miss much. "Yes, it was."

"You used to have the biggest crush on her when you were young."

"Like when I was nine or ten."

"From the time you were six you were smitten with the girl." She raised her brow in amusement and handed me a cookie.

"And what is that supposed to mean?"

Her expression sobered. She rested her hands on the counter and looked at me with worried eyes. "I think you might still have a crush on her, and I'm concerned."

"Mom! She's way out of my league. And besides, she's got a boyfriend."

"A married boyfriend. Like that's going to last."

"They seem happy enough together from what I hear."

"So, I have no need to worry?"

"Not at all."

"I'd love you to find a nice girl and settle down, but Kayla's not right for you. Even if she were available."

I agreed with her. On both counts. If I were honest, I still did have a crush on Kayla, especially after chatting with her yesterday. But she wasn't right for me. She didn't love the Lord, and her lifestyle was totally the opposite of mine. We had nothing in common. Plus, she wasn't available.

Mom finally accepted she had no need to worry, and the subject of Kayla was dropped. We began chatting about the Boys' Club. I told her about Ivan and how he'd dropped by yesterday and was eager to do some part-time work in the shop.

"You're doing great work with those boys. I'm so proud of you."

I smiled. My mother had always been supportive, especially

in the days after my accident when I'd gone on a downward spiral. It still grieved me when I thought about all that I'd put her and the rest of the family through. I couldn't have asked for better parents. But I knew she worried about me. Like she said, she'd love me to find someone to settle down with, but although I'd love that too, I'd accepted it might not ever happen, and that I might be single for the rest of my life. I was okay with that. I really did enjoy being alone in my workshop. Mainly because I wasn't alone; God was with me as I worked my clay, shaping it into what I had in mind for it, reminding me of what He was doing in my own life. He was taking something that had been messed up and bruised, a lump of dirt, basically, and was shaping me slowly and gently into what He'd intended me to be right from the beginning, before I was even a speck in my mother's womb. I was far from perfect, but I could sense that my anger and bitterness were slowly but surely being replaced with peace and contentment.

"Thanks. I really enjoy working with them."

"I know you do."

She patted my hand then gave me a container full of cookies. "For you."

"I thought they were for the boys."

"You're my special boy, Dane. Take them."

I laughed and popped a kiss on her cheek. "You're the best."

"Off with you. I've got work to do."

"I know when I'm not wanted." I was joking; she'd never kick me out if I wanted to stay, but I had work to do too.

Back in my workshop, I popped the container of cookies on the shelf where I kept my snacks and pulled up my sleeves, ready to make a new fruit bowl to replace the one Kayla had taken yesterday. She'd never said who it was for, and it made me wonder. It didn't seem like a gift she'd buy for her boyfriend. Maybe it was for her mom.

9

KAYLA

EPITAPH. *"Naked I came from my mother's womb, and naked I will depart. He gave and He has taken away."*

I HAD TROUBLE FALLING ASLEEP, and even when I did, my mind and body were restless. I had the strangest of dreams. I was at a funeral; my father's, to be exact. I stared at his open casket. He looked handsome in his favorite brown suit. Handsome but still. So still. I shivered and turned away.

His headstone was already in place. I strained to read it.

Stephen David McCormack.

Born January 12, 1963. Returned home September 13, 2017.

Beloved husband, father and grandfather.

Absent From The Body, Present With The Lord.

I heard a voice and was drawn back to the ceremony as Reverend Matthew began preaching.

"Stephen was a wonderful man, kind and generous to all. He

loved the Lord with his whole heart. He also loved his daughter, although he didn't like or approve of her lifestyle."

All eyes turned to me. I couldn't move.

"He may have lived had she chosen a different path."

Everyone gasped. I shook my head and backed away. It wasn't my fault he'd died; it was God's. Tears streamed down my cheeks. I screamed as his coffin was lowered into the ground.

I woke in a sweat. The dream had been so real. *It wasn't my fault my dad was sick; it was God's.* If He was so loving, He should have looked after him better. I had nothing to do with it.

I threw my covers off, jumped out of bed and snuck downstairs. I unlocked my car, climbed in and sped to the lake at the bottom of our street where I proceeded to drink my bottle of wine. The bowl I'd gotten earlier that day caught my attention. I was tempted to toss it out the window and let it smash to smithereens. Why did I even think my mom would like it? But I couldn't do it; Dane had put too much time and effort into making it. I finished my bottle instead.

My thoughts turned to Dane as I stared at the dark water stretching into the distance. The wine was going to my head, and a strange image of him and me wading into the water together flitted through my mind. I didn't think it was a memory from the past, but maybe it was. I barely remembered him. Maybe we had waded into the water together as kids—the lake used to be my favorite swimming place.

I sighed. What was I doing here, staring at this lake in the middle of nowhere, drinking on my own? It was a far cry from the bright lights of L.A., that was for sure. I'd try harder to convince Dad to come back with me. To get better treatment options. I didn't want to watch him lowered into the ground. And all that talk about God and heaven? It was just hopeful thinking as far as I was concerned. This life was all there was. Singing was my life, and I needed to get back to it. Back to my fans. Back to Gregor. I opened my phone. He still hadn't called. Although it was the middle of the night, I called him. I'd keep calling until he answered.

After the third time it diverted to voice-mail, I threw my phone out the window. It landed with a thud. I opened my door and fell face first into damp grass and closed my eyes. My phone could wait.

I woke to someone tapping my shoulder. "Are you all right, miss?"

I struggled to lift my head. When I did, my vision blurred as streaks of early morning sunlight shimmered on the lake, blinding me. I made out the figure of a boy. I blinked and covered my eyes. "Yes, I'm fine, thank you."

"You don't look fine. Is that your phone?"

My gaze followed the direction he was pointing. It looked like my phone, but what was it doing over there? "Probably."

"It was ringing."

My head jerked up. Maybe it was Gregor. I tried to give the boy a smile. "Thanks. I'll be fine."

He tipped his head and continued his early morning jog as I crawled to retrieve my phone. Once in my hand, I leaned against the side of the car and opened it. Yes, a missed call from Gregor! Less than two minutes ago. I quickly punched his number, expecting him to answer right away.

He answered after five rings. "*Ma chérie.* At last."

"Where are you?"

"In my apartment."

"You didn't return my calls."

"I have now."

I held my head to stop it spinning. "I miss you."

"And I miss you, too, *chérie*. I want to be with you."

"I want to be with you, too."

"Let me come."

"No. I'll be back soon."

"How is your father?"

"Sick." I almost said *dying,* but caught myself in time. "I'm trying to convince him to come back with me."

"Will he?"

"I don't know."

"I need to go to Paris next week."

I stiffened. Any time he mentioned Paris I immediately thought of his wife. "What for?"

"A new role."

"How long will you be gone?"

"I'm not sure. Come with me."

I groaned. Not again. "I can't, you know that."

"Let me know if you change your mind."

"Okay."

"I have to go. I love you."

"Say it in French." I clutched the phone.

"Je t'aime, ma chérie."

"I love you, too, Gregor."

After the call ended, unbidden tears welled in my eyes and ran down my cheeks. Maybe I should go to Paris after all. But how could I leave my dad after that dream? What if I left and it came true?

I wiped my cheeks and crawled into my car. I doubted I could sneak back inside without being noticed, but I'd try.

10

DANE

CLAY. *"Shall the potter be considered as equal with the clay? Or what is formed say to him who formed it, 'He has no understanding'?"*

I DIDN'T SEE Kayla for the next few days, but she was constantly in my thoughts and prayers. Late one afternoon, as daylight faded and the shadows from the large dogwood trees in our backyard drew longer, she poked her head into the workshop, taking me by surprise.

"May I come in?"

I smiled. "Sure." I slowed my wheel and walked to the basin to wash my hands. I'd been up to my elbows in mud, and it took a while to scrub it all off.

Kayla strolled over to the wheel. "What are you making?"

"Another pot." I laughed.

"Don't you ever get tired of making the same things?"

"Not really. Every pot I make is slightly different. I like giving them individual touches that make them unique."

She let out a heavy sigh. Something worried her.

"Can I get you a drink?"

"Coffee would be great, thank you. I guess you don't have anything stronger?"

"Sorry."

"Coffee it is."

I filled my ancient coffee machine with water and ground coffee beans and switched it on. I rarely used it as I had very few visitors and I preferred tea, but the pleasant aroma of brewing coffee could make me change my mind. "How have you been?"

She plonked onto a stool and crossed her arms on the counter. "Not so good."

"Why's that?"

"My dad's having surgery tomorrow."

"But that's good, isn't it? They might remove all the cancer?"

"Yes, but I'm worried they won't."

"He's a strong man, Kayla. If anyone can beat cancer, it's your father."

"I'd feel happier if he'd come back to L.A. with me. He'd get better treatment there."

"We've been through this, I believe."

"I know."

I filled two mugs with coffee and held up the sugar and cream.

"Just cream, thanks. I have to watch my weight."

"You're kidding, right?"

"Not at all. My manager makes me weigh myself every day. If I put on so much as an ounce, he puts me on a diet."

"But you're so thin."

She shook her head. "I'm not. I've put on weight already since being here."

"It must be your mother's cooking."

"Maybe."

"How's your dad feeling about the surgery?" I handed her the coffee and sat on a stool beside her, pinching myself that Kayla McCormack was actually in my workshop.

"He keeps saying he's okay. I don't know if he's being honest or not. I sometimes think that all the talk about trusting God is just a cover."

"I don't think it is." I sipped my coffee.

She shrugged and toyed with her mug. "You might be right."

We sat in silence for a few moments. I wondered what had really brought her to the other side of town.

"I'm going back next week."

My brow lifted. "So soon?"

She nodded. "My manager told me that if I don't go back and finish my tour, my fans will desert me."

"Surely not."

"I don't want to run the risk."

"I guess your boyfriend will be happy about you going back."

"He's in Paris."

"Oh." I didn't know what to say. I was out of my depth, never having had much to do with girls, especially one so famous as Kayla. And her boyfriend was even more so. I had no idea how these high-flyers lived. Nor did I want to. My simple life suited me just fine. "Will you come back to Shelton?"

"My parents want me to." She stared at her mug before looking up. "Why did you join the military?"

I blinked. I hadn't expected that. "I guess I thought it was a good thing to do."

"And was it?"

I thought about that for a moment, unsure of how much to tell her. I doubted she was ready for the whole story. "It changed my life."

"Because of your accident?"

"Partly. But I'd also changed before it happened."

"Are you going to tell me, or do I need to drag it out of you?"

I chuckled and wondered why she was so interested. Maybe it was to get her mind off her dad's surgery. "Okay, I'll tell you, if you want to hear."

"I do."

"You know how quiet I used to be at school?"

She nodded, a small smile growing on her face. She was so pretty when she smiled. "So quiet I couldn't even remember you, other than you tying my ribbons together and staring at me during the talent contest."

I laughed. It seemed such a long time ago. "All that changed when I joined up. I'm ashamed of it now, but when I got away from all I'd known, a whole new world opened up and I got led astray."

"I can't imagine that."

"You have to believe it. Quiet little Dane Carmichael became loud and aggressive. It was mainly the drink that did it. I didn't know how to handle it, and I drank more than I should. I forgot all I knew and believed about living a holy life and got dragged into fight after fight, until one of those fights indirectly caused the accident." I told her about my fight with my good friend Will, and then about how the plane had fallen on my leg because I wasn't concentrating. I paused before I told her about my suicide attempt.

Her mouth fell open. "I don't believe it. You didn't try to kill yourself."

"I did. I'm glad I didn't succeed, but I'm also glad I went through everything I did. God taught me so much through that time. He used those experiences to mold and shape me. If I hadn't joined up and had my accident, no doubt He would have used something else to grab my attention and teach me His ways. So, to answer your question, yes, it was a good thing."

Kayla drew a slow breath and toyed with her mug. "I killed someone once."

If she made the comment for shock value, she succeeded. I almost choked on my coffee. "You didn't."

She nodded. "I did. I had an abortion." There was a faint tremor in her voice, and I wondered why she would tell me this. It wasn't a normal thing to tell someone you barely knew, but she must have trusted me enough to confide in me. I needed to think quickly. "How long ago?"

"Eight years. My parents don't know. They'd never understand."

I quickly did the math. She would have been eighteen and in her first year away from home. "You must have been desperate."

"A baby would have ruined my career before it began." She blinked back tears.

I guess I understood that but choosing to have an abortion

wouldn't have been easy. And it seemed she still regretted it, which was a good thing; it showed she had a heart. And she knew what she'd done was wrong. I sensed she'd never forgiven herself. "We all make mistakes."

She shrugged. "It's in the past." She let out a wistful sigh.

It wasn't, but I'd let it go for now. "Would you like me to teach you to throw a pot?"

"Topic too heavy?"

"No, I just thought you could do with a distraction."

"Okay. I'm up for it. Show me what to do." She jumped off her stool and headed straight to the wheel.

Kayla followed my instructions carefully. She made a mess of it, of course, but she didn't give up until the clay began to take shape in her hands. I smiled at the look of wonder on her face. When our fingers touched once or twice, I was quick to move my hand away. I didn't want anything to spoil the friendship I felt was starting to take root. It was a pity she was returning to L.A. so soon.

"You've done a great job for your first attempt."

"It's not very round." She laughed.

"It doesn't matter. You made it, and you can be proud of it."

"But it's not quite the way I want it to be."

"You can keep shaping it."

"Okay. I don't need to be anywhere."

"Not even with your dad?"

She glanced at the time. "Yes, I should get home for dinner. Mom won't be happy if I'm not there."

"I can finish this off if you like."

"Would you? That would be great."

"It won't go into the kiln before you leave, but I'll have it waiting for you when you come back."

"Thank you, Dane. You're so sweet."

I was tempted to reply that she was so pretty, but I refrained. Instead, I chuckled. "You're welcome."

After she left, I finished shaping her pot, praying for her and her dad as I worked the clay. I didn't change the shape, I just tidied up some of the less rounded parts. It was Kayla's pot, after all. Lovingly made by her own hands, just like she was a precious creation of her Father in Heaven, even though she didn't know it.

11

KAYLA

ELATION. *"Hatred stirs up conflict, but love covers over all wrongs."*

As I DROVE AWAY from Dane's workshop, I felt in better spirits than I had all week. He was such an odd character. Quiet, deep, but something about him intrigued me. Maybe it was quiet confidence; he seemed to know who he was, and even though he had that troublesome leg, he seemed content with life. It amazed me.

I couldn't believe I'd told him about my abortion. I hadn't told anyone, not even Brady Johanson, my boyfriend at the time and the father of my baby. He didn't even know I was expecting. But after Dane had told me about his experiences, it seemed natural to share mine. I still hated myself for having that abortion, although I'd had no choice if I wanted a music career. Despite my parents thinking I hadn't learned anything from them, I knew it was wrong to kill an innocent baby, even if it was only a tiny fetus. God definitely would never give me a second chance. Not that I wanted Him to.

When I arrived back at my parents' house, my sister's car was parked in the driveway. The perfect daughter, Jennifer could do no wrong. And she'd given my parents a grandchild. If my mom knew what I'd done to the one I could have given them, she definitely would never have spoken to me again. If Jennifer was here, that meant Toby was here, too. At three years of age, Toby was the focus of my mother's attention. She doted on him, a little too much in my opinion, spoiling him rotten and giving him too much. But it was okay. I'd only seen him twice since being at home, but I'd already come to love him. And he seemed taken with me being a famous singer, although neither his mother nor his grandmother would let him listen to any of my songs. "He'll be damaged for life if he listens to your filth." Neither my sister nor my mother minced their words. My dad was a little more supportive. "I'm sure he'd love it if you grabbed your old guitar and sang a nice song for him. Maybe the one you sang at the talent contest.

I raised my brow. "Seriously, Dad? You want me to sing that song?"

"He's only three, sweetheart. I'm sure he'd like it."

At least Dad was sensitive and didn't say that Toby would be damaged for life if he heard any of my rock songs. My mother could be so hurtful.

Jennifer had obviously come for a family dinner before Dad's surgery. Great. Three of them to attack me. As if Mom and Adam weren't enough. At least Dad was more on my side these last few days. But no doubt I'd have to suffer through more trusting in God talk. If it wasn't for him, I'd be out of there in a flash.

Dinner was as expected. Even though Dad should have been the focus of attention, since he was undergoing major surgery the following day, they all took great joy in telling me how terrible I was. Jennifer had even read up on Gregor's past and smugly told me how many children he had. I'd never met Gregor's children, but I knew about them. Two boys and a girl from his first wife, Fleur, two boys from a relationship he said he'd rather forget, and one daughter with his wife, Danielle. I hoped that one day we'd have a child together. But I wasn't ready yet. I couldn't give up my career to have a baby. Just like I couldn't have given up my dreams eight years ago when I discovered I was pregnant.

I ignored Jennifer and chatted with Toby and Dad.

Finally, dinner was over. But then came a prayer time. I groaned when Adam asked us all to gather around Dad to pray for him. Not that I didn't want to wish Dad all the best, but I really thought all this praying a waste of time. Unless I wanted to cause a scene, I had no choice. I stood with my mother and my brother and sister and placed my hand on Dad's shoulder. I listened to them all pray one at a time and was glad when they didn't wait for me to follow suit. They would have been waiting all night. Instead, I leaned down and gave Dad a big hug. "I'll be thinking about you, Dad, and I'll be waiting when you come out."

He smiled at me and returned my hug. "Thanks, Kayla. I appreciate that." He hugged the others as well. I offered to clean up to avoid listening to more God talk. Jennifer said she needed to get Toby home to bed, but promised to be at the hospital bright and early. Her husband, Jack, was an interstate trucker and was out of town for the week.

Mom joined me in the kitchen as I wiped the counter down. "I wish you weren't leaving."

"I've still got a few days before I go."

"I know, but your father needs you here."

"He's got you, and Adam and Jennifer."

"Yes, but he has a soft spot for you, Kayla. I don't know why."

"Thank you," I replied sarcastically.

"Why do you have to go back to Los Angeles? Haven't you earned enough money?"

"It's not about the money, Mom. I love what I do. And I can't keep postponing my tour indefinitely."

"After the tour?"

"Maybe. I'll have to see what Gregor's doing. I guess he's still not welcome?"

"What do you think?"

I leaned against the counter and held her gaze. "I honestly don't see why not. You haven't even met him. What if we get married? Will he be welcome then?"

Mom drew a long breath and pursed her lips. "He'd have to get divorced first."

"He's planning on it."

Her shoulders sagged. "You're not going to marry him, are you?"

"And if I were?"

"I… I guess we'd have to re-think it."

"So why can't you re-think it now? He doesn't have to stay here. He could stay in a hotel." I thought I'd better not say I'd join him.

My mother grew quiet. "Do you love him?"

"Yes."

"Let me talk with your father."

My eyes widened. I didn't see that coming. "Okay."

I finished wiping the counter and then dried the big dishes that didn't fit into the dishwasher and wondered what Dad would say. I guessed he'd be okay with it if Mom was. I doubted Gregor could come since he was in Paris on a new shoot, but there was no harm in asking. I chuckled when I thought about what the townsfolk would think having such a famous movie star arrive in their little old town. Having me here had kept the tongues wagging enough as it was.

Mom returned a few moments later. "Your father said he's welcome if he stays in a hotel."

Without thinking, I threw my arms around her and kissed her cheek. "Thanks. I'll go call him."

Gregor didn't answer, which didn't surprise me. He rarely answered when I called, and he called back when he could. I didn't want to wait so I sent a text. I had to word it carefully, as I didn't want him to know the real reason I'd come alone in the first place.

Hi sweetie. Dad's having a major operation and I'd love for you to come if you can, but I'll understand if you can't. I know it's short notice, but I really miss you and want you here with me. I love you. Call me when you can. Kayla.

Several moments later, my phone dinged.

Ma chérie! Of course I'll come. I'll cancel my shoot and catch the first plane out. I'll see you soon.

I don't know why he didn't call, but it didn't matter. Gregor was coming!

He caught an overnight flight and arrived the next morning. I collected him from the airport but we arrived at the hospital five minutes too late; my dad was already in surgery. Mom was polite but Adam and Jennifer both shot daggers at us. Their rudeness shocked me. I didn't care, Gregor was here and that was all that mattered.

12

DANE

RESTRAINT. *"Like a city whose walls are broken through is a person who lacks self-control."*

THE FOLLOWING MORNING, I decided to go to the hospital to see if Kayla could do with any support. I'd sent her a text after I finished shaping her pot the night before and attached a photo of it. She sent a text back and thanked me. We kept texting for a while, which was quite a strange thing for me to do. I'd never played this game before, but it seemed she had. She was as quick as lightning with her responses, but it took me forever. It was a strange conversation, as if she were chatting with a best friend.

Her: If you could eat just one food for an entire year, what would it be?

Me: Chocolate. What about you?

Her: Marshmallows.

Me: That's not food. I couldn't help but smile. *Why are you asking me about food, anyway?*

Her: Would you laugh if I told you I was playing a game on my phone?

Me: That depends. What is it?

Her: Scrabble.

Me: I'm disappointed, because I thought it would be something fun.

Her: It is, maybe I'll teach you one day.

Me: I'm not a nerd.

Her: Yes you are. A nice one.

I was tempted to take offense. Why would she call me a nerd? If she was playing scrabble on her own, she was the nerd, not me. How did that happen? I laughed. What did it matter? Kayla and I were chatting like best friends. Maybe this was part of God's plan.

Me: Goodnight. I'll be praying the operation goes well.

I waited longer than normal for a reply. Finally, one came. It was brief. All she said was 'Thankyou'.

So why hadn't she told me that her boyfriend was coming? Not that it mattered. I smiled and shook his hand when she introduced us and tried not to let my confusion show. The guy had a firm handshake. I reciprocated. I wasn't going to let him think he had the upper-hand on me. Kayla was clinging to him like a drowning man would cling to a life buoy. He was good-looking, I'd give him that much, but he seemed too smooth with his French accent and all. I guessed he couldn't help that, he was French after all, but he seemed smarmy. I hoped he wouldn't hurt Kayla. He'd have me to answer to if he did. That thought shocked me as we didn't know each other that well, but I felt she needed protecting from playboys like Gregor

DuBois. Although to be fair, he'd done nothing to me, and as a Christian I knew I should show him Christian love.

After exchanging a few forced pleasantries and asking how her father was, I excused myself, saying I needed to get back to work. Stephen was still in surgery and would be for another few hours. I said I'd check back later.

I didn't need to go to back to work. Ivan was looking after the shop for me; once again, I hadn't asked why he wasn't in school. I knew I'd have to one day soon, or else I could get into trouble for encouraging him to skip. Instead of returning right away, I used the time to prepare for Boys' Club that afternoon.

The hall where we met adjoined the church sanctuary. Being a weekday, the sanctuary was empty, although the door was open for anyone who wanted to go inside and pray. I'd always thought this a little unusual, as Jesus encouraged His followers to pray wherever they were. I guessed some people felt closer to God if they were in a church building, especially one as nice as this, with its stained-glass windows and old timber pews. I was happy to pray anywhere. Prayer was just talking to God, although it was good to show Him respect, being the God of the universe and all.

I'd been thinking through what I should share with the boys this afternoon. I felt strongly that I needed to continue on from last time as it was such an important issue. How *do* you maintain Christian standards in a world that has lost its way and where almost anything goes? Before I opened my note-book and Bible, I bowed my head and prayed.

"Dear Lord, please guide me as I prepare this study. You know how important this matter is, and how I long for these boys to understand as well. But more than that, dear Lord, I want them to truly know what it is to live for You. To be so in love with You that nothing will lure them away from serving You as they grow into adulthood. Help them become strong men of God, filled with Your Spirit, washed in Your blood. Lord, I'm just Your humble servant, but I thank You for the opportunity of ministering to them. Please give me wisdom and insight to reach them for You and to encourage them to grow in Your ways. And dear Lord, I pray also for Kayla and her family. Be with Stephen and the surgeons right now. Thank You that he's trusting in You, and I pray that Kayla might also do the same one day. In Jesus' precious name. Amen."

I raised my head and got the shock of my life. Mrs. Steward stood about three feet from me. She quickly wiped tears from her eyes and sat beside me. "Dane, that was the most beautiful prayer. The boys are blessed to have you as their mentor."

I smiled at the old woman and thanked her, but wondered why she'd been listening to a private prayer.

"I'm sorry if I startled you. I was preparing some refreshments for this afternoon's Bible study and thought I heard someone, so I popped in to see who it was."

"I thought I was alone, but no matter. I came in to prepare for Boys' Club."

"We've all been praying for Stephen. Such a major operation. I heard that boyfriend of his daughter arrived this morning. I'm surprised he was welcome after those photos in yesterday's paper."

"What photos?" I asked without thinking.

"You didn't see them?"

I was tempted to say that I wouldn't be asking if I had, but I bit my tongue. I was also tempted to ask why she was reading gossip magazines and papers in the first place, but I didn't. Instead I just said I hadn't.

"He was photographed in Paris with his wife. I wonder what young Kayla has to say about that!"

A heavy lump landed in my stomach. The guy was smarmy, but I didn't think he'd do this to Kayla. She obviously didn't know. Or if she did, she was covering it up very well. 'There has to be an explanation."

"Not according to the paper. They say they're planning to reconcile. Which they should. They're husband and wife, after all."

"You can't believe everything you read in the paper, Mrs. Steward."

"I know that, Dane, but there could be truth in it."

"Well, maybe it's best not to say too much before we know how true it is. For Kayla's sake. And her parents'."

She pursed her lips. I could see how difficult that would be for her. She'd be wanting to tell everyone she met. She let out a heavy sigh. "I'll try."

"And I'll try to find out if it's true or not."

"I'd be giving her a wide berth. She's bad news."

I sucked in a slow breath and prayed for patience. Mrs. Steward didn't know Kayla. She didn't know what was going on inside her heart. I didn't either, but God did, and I sensed He was working really hard on her.

"She's a child of God, Mrs. Steward. She's just wandered off the path for a while. I have every confidence she'll find her way back one day soon." I didn't want to offend her, but I wouldn't allow her to put Kayla down like that.

"I think you have a crush on her, Dane. Be careful."

"You're wrong. But she *is* my friend."

She raised a brow and patted my shoulder. "I must be getting on. The refreshments won't prepare themselves."

"And neither will my study."

After she left, I opened my Bible to Colossians chapter 3, verses 12 to 14. I felt this passage would be the most appropriate one to use as the base for our discussions, and as I read it, I knew it was perfect.

Therefore, as God's chosen people, holy and dearly loved, clothe yourselves with compassion, kindness, humility, gentleness and patience. Bear with each other and forgive one another if any of you has a grievance against someone. Forgive as the Lord forgave you. And over all these virtues put on love, which binds them all together in perfect unity.

The boys first needed to know who they were in Christ. They needed to be grounded and rooted in their faith, and then they needed to clothe themselves with the fruit of the Spirit. But they had to choose to do this. They had to want it. I began scribbling notes, adding questions and thoughts as they came to mind. After an hour or so, I felt ready for this afternoon's meeting.

I glanced at my watch. I'd told Ivan I'd be back by lunchtime, so I packed my things and headed to my car. As I drove past the hospital, I wondered how Stephen was, but thoughts of Kayla and Gregor dominated my mind. Did she know about those photos? And if so, how was she feeling about them? Would he deny the rumors? Because that's all they'd no doubt be. Rumors and gossip.

I'd read further into Colossians when I was doing my preparation, and verse 8 really hit me between my eyes: *But now you must also rid yourselves of all such things as these: anger, rage, malice, slander, and filthy language from your lips.* I was just as guilty as Mrs. Steward. I'd struggled to contain my anger and annoyance when I saw Gregor with Kayla, just as Mrs. Steward struggled with gossip. I shouldn't judge her. We were all guilty before God. Once again I repented and thanked Him for the cleansing blood of Jesus. He still had a long way to go with me, but I was so thankful for His patience and understanding.

13

KAYLA

RELAPSE. *"The spirit is willing, but the flesh is weak."*

GREGOR CHECKED his phone for like the thousandth time in ten minutes. When I peered across him to see the screen, he turned it away from me.

"Are you hiding something?"

"Of course not, *ma chérie.*" He kissed the top of my head, but then looked at the phone again.

"Put it away, then. Talk with me." I didn't want to be upset with him; he'd traveled through the night to get here, and he had no real reason to come, other than I'd asked him to. But now he was here, I wanted him to be *really* here. With me. Not with whomever was on the other end of his phone.

"I'm sorry. I've been rude." He slipped it into his pocket and faced me, tucking some loose strands of hair behind my ear. "What do you want to talk about?"

"What have you been doing in Paris?" As soon as the words

came out, I wished I could take them back. His face flinched, and if I wasn't mistaken, a look of alarm flashed across it before he composed himself.

"Oh, you know, just the normal. Meetings, filming, you know how it goes."

I didn't, but if Lawrence had his way, I'd be doing the same when I returned. He'd been hassling me every day about whether I was planning to accept the offer to be a lead actor in a new YA movie. I wasn't excited about it in any shape or form, but he desperately wanted me to do it. I assumed money was his motivating force. "Kind of. Have you seen your daughter?"

He flinched again, making me wonder if he was ill.

I rubbed his arm. "Are you okay?"

"A bit jet-lagged. I think I should go to the hotel for a while if that's all right."

"I'll come with you."

"What about your father?"

"It could be hours before he's out of surgery."

"Okay, I'd love you to come." He looked at me slowly and seductively, making my insides melt. I hoped my mother hadn't noticed. I leaned across my other side and told her I'd be back soon; I was just showing Gregor to his hotel. She didn't say anything, but her narrowed eyes and pursed lips spoke volumes.

I felt like a naughty schoolgirl as Gregor and I slipped away together. We ducked out the back entrance to avoid prying eyes and jumped into my rental car. I'd booked the best hotel in town, 'The Lakeside', but I cringed as I pulled into the parking lot. Compared to the fancy hotels in Paris, this was a dump. I glanced over at him. "I'm sorry, this was the best I could do."

"It's okay, *ma chérie*. At least we can be alone."

I smiled and felt somewhat relieved, although I thought he was probably just trying to make me feel better. I also felt relieved that he still wanted me.

We checked in, ignoring the inquisitive looks of the staff, and fell into each other's arms as Gregor kicked the door shut. He kissed me urgently and passionately. I responded, trying to block out all thought of what my parents would say. Or what God would say. I needed Gregor's love more than anything in the world. But I couldn't do it. I pushed him away. "I'm sorry, Gregor, I can't."

He pulled me back, nuzzling my neck. *"Ma chérie*, what's the matter?"

I pushed him away again and sighed. "I can't do this while my dad's in the hospital. I'm sorry. You must understand." I began buttoning my shirt.

He flopped back onto the bed and let out a frustrated sigh. I felt bad, but I couldn't do it.

Just then my phone buzzed. I reached onto the floor and picked it up. It was Mom. I was so grateful she didn't do Face-time. I answered quickly. "Mom, has Dad come out of surgery?"

"Yes. I thought you'd be back by now."

"I'm on my way. How is he?" I scooted off the bed and slipped my shoes on.

"Groggy, but the surgeon seems optimistic."

"That's great. That's so great." I breathed a sigh of relief. My dad wasn't going to die.

"He still has a long way to go to be clear of it."

I knew that. He still needed radiation treatment and there was no guarantee the cancer wouldn't return in the future. But against all odds, this was a good start. Maybe all that praying had worked. I'd never tell my mom I'd thought that; I'd never hear the end of it.

I gave Gregor a big hug and kiss. "I'll be back soon."

"Have you changed your mind?" He stroked my hair and looked into my eyes.

"About staying?"

He nodded.

"You know I can't, but we can have dinner together."

"Okay. See you soon, *chérie.*"

I gave him another kiss and left, although my heart was heavy. Gregor was not amused that I'd left him hanging.

I PUSHED MY HEAVINESS ASIDE. Dad was going to be okay. As I drove back to the hospital, I belted out my favorite song, tapping my fingers on the wheel and pretending I was playing to thousands. I pulled up at a set of traffic lights, one of the few in the whole of Shelton. A newspaper stand on the sidewalk caught my attention. It was one of those trashy papers, put out to grab the attention of passers-by, but the photo on the front cover was as clear as day. Gregor Dubois and his wife, cozying up together in Paris. My heart plummeted. It had to be some kind of joke. The paper had it wrong. It was an old story; Gregor hadn't been seeing his wife. He loved me.

The lights changed to green and I pulled away in a daze feeling sick to my stomach. Gregor wouldn't do this to me, would he? *Would he?* I brushed tears from my eyes as I yanked the wheel and did a U-turn. My tires screeched but I didn't care. I had to confront him. I needed to know. My dad would have to wait.

Gregor was asleep when I opened the door to the hotel room. I stepped inside and closed the door quietly. I needed time to think. My stomach was still clenched tight as I stood staring at him, my hands and lips trembling. Would this be the end of my happy ever after? It couldn't be. He'd told me a million times how much he loved me, how he'd divorce his wife and marry me as soon as he could. I had no reason to doubt him... until that photo.

His phone on the night stand caught my attention. I went to grab it but stopped myself. How would I explain it if he woke and caught me scrolling through his messages? No, it was better to ask him outright.

He must have sensed my presence, because he rolled over and opened his eyes. "*Ma chérie!* Have I been asleep that long? You're back already."

"I didn't make it to the hospital." I tried to keep my voice even, but my lip quivered.

He straightened against the pillows and held his arms out. "Come to bed, my darling. You look upset."

"No." I swallowed hard. Normally I wouldn't have thought twice, but I had to be firm.

"What's the matter? Has something happened to your father?"

"Not that I know of. I saw a newspaper with the photo of you and your wife in Paris."

"Photo?" For a moment, he looked as if he was going to deny it. Then he said, "Oh." His face fell. "I was going to tell you about that."

I raised my brows and stood my ground. "Well?"

"It's nothing, *ma chérie*. You know what the media do... they snap one shot and sensationalize it to sell papers."

"So it's nothing to be worried about? You're not seeing your wife again?"

"I did see her, but only to talk about the divorce."

"You looked close." Too close. They had their arms around one another.

'We're not enemies."

"That's not what you told me."

"We need to be amicable for our daughter's sake."

I narrowed my eyes. Should I believe him?

"Come here." He extended his arms again. I so wanted to believe him. "You're my girl. My beautiful feisty girl. *Je t'aime, ma chérie.*"

I wanted to go to him, to be held by him, to be loved by him. But something stopped me. My chest burned. I couldn't believe I was doing this. For the second time today, I wondered if what I was doing was wrong. If my parents might be right after all. The thought pierced my insides like a hot rod, but I remained firm. "No, I need to see my father. He's expecting me. I hope you're telling me the truth."

"Of course I am. I wouldn't lie to you, *chérie.*"

I wanted to ask him if he talked to his wife like that, but I bit my tongue. Had I been hoodwinked by his smooth talk? I wanted to think I was smarter than that, but I wasn't so sure. I forced a smile and stepped forward, placing a small kiss on his cheek, not the passionate kiss I'd given him earlier. "I need to see my father. I'll be back soon."

He grabbed my hand as I straightened, his dark eyes serious. "I'll come with you. Give me a minute." He slipped out of bed and pulled on his trousers. I forced myself not to allow the sight of his muscular chest to sway my resolve and was very relieved when he put his shirt on. I was glad he was coming with me. It gave me hope that he really did love me and wanted to be with me. And it might prevent me from doing anything stupid, like getting drunk.

I glanced at him as I pulled out of the parking lot. He had a generous mouth and classically handsome, dark features, but I was starting to realize that of more importance was whether he was trustworthy and loyal. If he was lying to me about his wife, I would never forgive him. "What did she say?"

His forehead puckered momentarily as he angled his head. "You mean about the divorce?"

I nodded. Of course that's what I meant. What else?

"It won't be a problem."

My shoulders sagged. They were Gregor's words, not hers, but I decided not to push him as we passed the stand with the newspaper. I tried to keep my eyes pointed straight ahead, but the paper stand was like a magnet. In my peripheral vision, I saw Gregor glance that way. He didn't say anything. I wondered how many other people in town had seen the photo. Probably everyone. He'd have some explaining to do with my family. *And with Dane.*

I felt so bad about him this morning. I'd been almost rude when he arrived unexpectedly, but I'd been so excited to see Gregor, and then I felt awkward introducing them. Not that there was anything to feel awkward about. Dane was just a friend. But I did feel bad.

We arrived at the hospital soon after. Gregor took my hand as we walked through the double doors and into the main reception area. I wanted to go in the back way to avoid attention, but he didn't seem worried about drawing attention to himself. Maybe it was his way of showing me he didn't care what people thought.

I kept my head straight, but I was aware that everyone's eyes were on us. We headed to the surgical ward. Mom had told me what room Dad was in, so we didn't stop to ask. She, Adam and Jennifer were all gathered around his bed, and they all looked up as we entered. Mom looked rather annoyed. I'd forgotten to tell her I'd been held up and that Gregor was coming back with me. I probably should have thought about it. It was just another mistake.

I ignored her, let go of Gregor's hand, stepped forward, and kissed Dad. "How are you feeling?" I smiled at him and studied his face. He'd only been out of surgery a short while and was no doubt still groggy from the anesthetic, but his eyes looked brighter. Maybe I was imagining it, trying to convince myself he looked better already. I don't know, but I was happy to see him awake and smiling.

He hadn't met Gregor, having already been in surgery when he arrived. It wasn't the ideal time to make the introduction, but it had to be done. "I've got someone I'd like you to meet." I glanced around and motioned for Gregor to come closer. My brother scowled but made way for him. "Dad, this is Gregor. Gregor, this my dad, Stephen."

They exchanged pleasantries, but I sensed the awkwardness. My dad was polite. That was all I could expect.

We didn't stay long; Dad needed to sleep. Mom said she'd stay with him for a bit. Adam had errands to run and Jennifer needed to collect Toby from a friend's place. Gregor wanted me to go back to the hotel with him. I said no, I wanted to go home and cook a nice meal for Mom.

He raised a brow. He knew I couldn't cook.

"You can help if you like."

He chuckled. He knew what that meant. I'd actually be

helping him. It didn't matter, as long as we were together, doing something to stop me continually wondering if he was trustworthy or not.

On the way home, I took a different route. I had no desire to ever see that photo again.

14

DANE

CLEANSING. *"Search me, God, and know my heart."*

I STOPPED at the store on my way home and saw the photo Mrs. Steward had told me about. They sure looked close. Too close for a couple divorcing. My heart went out to Kayla. No doubt she'd seen it by now, or at least heard about it. And no doubt Gregor would be trying to convince her it meant nothing. I hoped for her sake it didn't, but to be honest, I felt she'd be better off without him. But she'd have to come to that realization herself. If she were like me, it might take something catastrophic for her to realize the error of her ways. I hoped not. And that was the exact same hope I held for the boys. That they might live their lives without making terrible mistakes.

I chose not to buy the paper. I didn't need to read what was no doubt partial truth twisted and turned so much that no one would know what the truth was. But people would believe it anyway, truth or not.

After purchasing the few items I needed for lunch, I climbed back into my car and blinked. Kayla's car sped past with Gregor in the passenger seat, headed in the direction of the hospital. Last I knew, they'd been at the hospital. I assumed they'd gone out for something and tried not to think what that might be.

Ivan was busy tidying shelves when I arrived back at the shop. He seemed happy enough puttering about, so I left him to it while I made lunch. I promised him another turn on the wheel after we'd eaten, so he didn't waste any time wolfing down his roast beef sandwich.

He was eager to make a set of mugs for his mother. I told him he should start with a simple pot. He was happy with that. I got out some fresh clay and showed him how to wedge it, much like kneading bread dough, to remove air bubbles and any impurities remaining after the cleaning process, such as tiny slivers of wood, seeds, or stones that might be hidden, but could cause disaster when placed into the kiln if not found beforehand. Under such intense heat, impurities like these could cause the pot to explode, often damaging the other pots around it.

"It looks clean," Ivan said as he began the wedging process, mimicking my hand movements.

I laughed. "It does, but you'll be surprised how much rubbish is still lurking. It's important to spend time now to remove as much as possible to avoid problems further on." I chuckled to myself. This was exactly what I'd planned to discuss with the boys that afternoon. As we worked the raw clay, I prayed that this truth would resonate with the boys in general, and with Ivan in particular.

We continued working the clay until it was clean and

smooth, and with uniform texture. "Now we fix the clay to the wheel." I took my piece and smacked it with one swift, deliberate movement into the middle of the flat surface of the wheel. "It has to be completely attached and centered before you can do anything with it."

Ivan did the same on the spare wheel I had in the workshop. I smiled at him and encouraged him to keep going. "That's good. Keep it centered. Now wet your hands and increase the speed."

As I encouraged and guided him, Ivan's piece of clay slowly took shape. Eventually it looked like a pot. He slowed the wheel and I demonstrated again how to slide it off and onto a tray. "You did well, today. Now we'd better clean up and get ready for Boys' Club."

"I can't make it today."

My shoulders fell. I couldn't keep the disappointment from my voice. "That's a pity. Are you sure?"

He nodded. "I need to look after my little brothers."

I didn't want to be nosy and ask where his mom was going, but I did ask how old they were.

"Three and four. They're half-brothers."

I was starting to get a picture of Ivan's life. I didn't want to make assumptions as I knew they were often wrong, but at least I knew a little more.

"We'll miss you."

"I wanted to come."

I smiled and patted him gently on the back. "Next week?"

"Hopefully." He finished washing his hands and dried them on a towel. "I need to go. I told Mom I'd be home by four."

"I can drop you home. Your bike will fit in my pickup."

"Would you? That would be great."

"Yes, no problem. Let me clean up; I'll be just a few minutes."

"I'll help."

"Thanks." I smiled, appreciating Ivan's willingness to give.

Within minutes, the workshop was clean and tidy and we were loading his bicycle into the back of my pickup. We drove along in silence a short way, and then I asked the question I'd been trying not to. "Is your father still around?"

"Nuh. Never knew him."

"Oh." That was sad. Fathers play such an important role in their children's lives. I'd been blessed to have a great one. "What about your step-father?" I probably shouldn't have been asking these questions, but I sensed stuff was going on in Ivan's life that he might need help with, and knowing I was interested might help him share. Not that I had all the answers, but I knew Someone who did.

"Yeah, he's around." Ivan sounded less than enthusiastic. In fact, he slunk down in the seat and stared at his hands.

"You don't get along?"

"You could say that."

"If you want to talk, I'm a good listener."

"Nothing to talk about."

I gave him an encouraging smile. "That's okay. But if there is…"

"There's not. Just drop me here. I can ride the rest of the way."

My brows came together. "Are you sure? It's not a problem to drive you the whole way."

"Yeah, I'm sure. You won't want to drive down my street."

"Oh." I realized then that he was ashamed of where he lived, and I didn't blame him. Most folks in Shelton took pride in their homes, but it was well known that the residents of Elm Street vied for the prize of worst house.

I pulled over and turned to him. "I mean it, Ivan. If ever you want to talk, I'm here."

"Thanks. I'll be okay."

I drew a slow breath. My heart ached for him. He might not want to talk, but I was convinced stuff was going on that was messing with him. "Can I pray for you?"

He shrugged. "If you want."

I did want. I rested my hand lightly on his shoulder and closed my eyes. "Dear Lord, I pray for my friend, Ivan. Please bless him and let him know that You love him. That You're a good Father and that You only want the best for him. Be with him now as he takes care of his little brothers. Wrap your arms around him, dear Lord, and fill him with your peace. In Jesus' precious name. Amen."

"Amen."

I smiled at him again. God was working in Ivan's heart, and I prayed that the day would come soon when he would open it fully. "Take care. I'll see you again soon."

"Yeah. Thanks." He jumped out and grabbed his bike from the back. As I drove off, I waved and sent up another prayer.

I ARRIVED a few minutes before the boys began strolling in. They walked from school and were always ready for their afternoon feast. I was so grateful to the church ladies who faithfully prepared this food, freeing me to prepare their spiritual nourishment.

After they'd eaten, they split into groups as usual; some to play half-court basketball, others to play ping-pong, and still others just sat around and chilled out. They were good boys from church families, but I'd been one of them, and I knew that unless they were fully grounded in their faith, they could easily fall away and be lured by the trappings of the world, as I had been. I thought I was strong enough to withstand the pressure, but the things I'd been taught hadn't changed my heart enough, and I found that just like the raw clay Ivan and I had worked earlier that afternoon, all sorts of bad things lurked there. When the heat turned up, I'd exploded.

But it was hard; they thought they knew everything. I guess it was typical of teenagers. I prayed I could reach them, that God would give me the right words that would touch their hearts and help them understand the importance of what they were hearing. The importance of guarding their hearts and growing in the ways of the Lord, allowing Him to weed out all impurities so that when troubles came, as no doubt they would, their hearts and minds would be resolute and they would shine for God.

When they gathered on their bean bags soon after, I smiled and told them how glad I was to see them all. I was saddened that Ivan wasn't among them and prayed silently that all was well with him. "Today we're continuing with our theme of how to live for Jesus in a world that shuns His ways. Let's open in prayer." I bowed my head. "Dear Lord, please let Your words touch each of us deep inside today, so that we can shine for You in a world that has lost its way. Teach us Lord how to follow You. Amen."As usual, a round of *Amens* followed. "Let's open our Bibles to Colossians chapter 3. Can someone read for us?"

Chad offered and began reading. When he got to verse 8, I felt God telling me to share with them about the clay that Ivan and I had worked that afternoon, and I remembered I had a new box of clay in my pickup that I hadn't taken into my workshop. My heart quickened as I felt the leading of the Spirit. It could make such a difference if, instead of simply telling these boys about the need to remove impurities from their lives, they could see and feel the impurities in the clay, and I could explain to them the consequences of not removing them before being placed into the kiln.

"Chill for a bit. I need to get something."

They all looked at me quizzically as I wriggled out of my beanbag.

"Need any help?" a boy called Jared asked.

I was about to say that I was okay, but it was good for the boys to be helpful and to show kindness, so I smiled and said, "Yes, thank you."

Jared carried the box of clay inside and set it on the floor. I thanked him and proceeded to open it. "You all know that I make pots. And I know that some of you have done pottery at school, but I thought I'd give you all a chance to see what raw clay looks and feels like." I cut off chunks and handed them out. I also laid a large sheet of plastic I'd found in a cupboard onto the floor.

"You all think this clay looks clean, right?"

The boys all nodded.

"But it's rough, and if you look really carefully, you'll see tiny stones and pieces of twigs. Place your lump on the plastic and take a look."

They followed my instructions, and as each boy found a piece of debris and held it up, they were spurred on to find as many as they could.

I asked them what they thought might happen if this debris

remained in the clay when it was placed into the kiln. Some already knew, but others were surprised.

We reread Colossians chapter 3, verse 8. *"But now you must also rid yourselves of all such things as these: anger, rage, malice, slander, and filthy language from your lips."*

"There's also another verse I want to read, 2nd Corinthians chapter 7, verse 1. *Therefore, since we have these promises, dear friends, let us purify ourselves from everything that contaminates body and spirit, perfecting holiness out of reverence for God.* Why do you think this is so important?"

They grew thoughtful. Finally, Chad raised his hand. "So we can live the way God wants us to when things get bad."

"Perfect answer, Chad. Even though when we give our lives to the Lord and He no longer sees our sins because of Jesus' blood, it takes a lifetime for Him to work the impurities out of our lives. The more we allow Him to knead and mould our hearts, the cleaner we become on the inside, so that when we face troubles, we won't react with anger and rage, but with patience, humility and love. Like David prayed in the Psalms, we need to ask God to search our hearts, and to cleanse us of all impurities that we might live a holy life. I'd like us to pray and ask God to do just that. I know you've all asked Jesus into your lives, so this is just a deepening commitment. Will you pray with me?"

They all nodded and bowed their heads. I waited for a moment to allow them to settle, and then I began. "Lord God, You know I love You and want to live for You, but I ask You now to search my heart. I know that although I'm pure in Your sight, inside me lurks all sorts of bad things. Please search my heart and show me what I need to give to You so that I can live the holy life You've called me to live. In Jesus' name. Amen."

Silence filled the room and I sensed that the boys were all doing business with God. One by one they prayed aloud, asking God to touch their hearts and to show them what they needed to hand over to Him. Their desire to live a holy life gladdened my heart immensely.

Afterwards, Jared told me he'd cheated on a test at school, and that he was going to tell his teacher tomorrow. Tears sprang to my eyes. He said it was only a small test, but as he was praying, he knew that what he'd done was wrong and that God wanted him to make it right. Another boy told me he'd lied to his mom, and that he was going home to apologize. God was indeed working in these boys' hearts, and it humbled me so much. Once again, I felt so sad that Ivan hadn't been here, but his time would come. Maybe he wasn't quite ready for such soul searching.

As I drove home a short time later, I hummed along with the songs of praise I often played in my car and prayed that each of the boys, as well as myself, would hold fast to what we'd learned today.

15

KAYLA

RESOLVE. *"Do what is right, not what is easy."*

I SENSED Gregor's surprise as I pulled into the driveway of my parents' neat but small home.

"This is nice."

I laughed. "Why don't you say what you really think!"

"It's quaint, *chérie*. It's nice."

"It might be, but it's tiny."

"Does it matter?"

"Not really. I assumed you'd think my parents lived in a mansion since I'm a famous pop-star. I know your mother lives in a villa."

He shrugged. "Your parents must like it."

"They do." I'd given up trying to get them to move. I turned the ignition off and opened my door. A curtain in the window of the house opposite ruffled. Another nosy neighbor. I sighed. I'd be glad to get back to LA. I led the way up the steps and unlocked the door. The house had a distinctive smell; not offensive so much as worn in.

I was very aware of Gregor behind me as we walked down the hallway. He slipped his arms around me from behind and nuzzled my neck. "How about it, *chérie?*"

I arched my back against him. Everything within me wanted him, *but not in this house*. I turned around and wrapped my arms around his neck, looking deep into his bluer than blue eyes. "We can't, Gregor. My mother would be horrified if she found out."

"You're not a child, Kayla."

"No, but it would be wrong." And I couldn't put the photo out of my mind.

"You said you didn't care what your parents thought." The feather-touch of his lips across mine weakened my knees. I almost gave in, but gently pushed him away.

"I'm sorry. Besides, my brother could be home any time. And we need to cook, remember?"

He let out a frustrated sigh. "Show me the kitchen."

I turned around and walked the short distance to the back of the house, tossing my keys and purse onto the kitchen counter. "Would you like a drink?"

"Red wine?"

"Not in this house, sorry. Tea, coffee, or Coke."

"Guess it's a Coke."

I opened the fridge and took out two bottles, handing him one. Red wine would have been better.

"What are we cooking?"

I shrugged. "Not sure what Mom's got." I proceeded to check the fridge, freezer and pantry. Lots of stuff but I had no idea what most of it was.

"Let me look?"

"Please, go ahead." I was starting to think that cooking a special meal for Mom and Adam was a bad idea. We should have just grabbed a take-out, so I suggested it.

"Whatever you think, Kayla." He was beginning to sound annoyed. I guess it was to be expected. The famous Gregor DuBois trying to find something decent to cook in a tiny house in a back-water town. What had I been thinking?

"Let's get take-out."

I picked up my phone, about to call the local Chinese restaurant, when a message popped up. It was from Dane. I clicked on it, scanning it quickly.

Just checking to see how your father is. I hope he's doing well. Also hoping you're okay. Thinking of you, Dane.

"All okay?" Gregor asked.

I nodded, swallowing hard. "Just a friend checking on my dad." I'd read between the lines and knew that Dane had seen the photo.

"The cripple?"

My eyes widened. "He's not a cripple!"

"Sure looked like it to me."

"He's a really nice person."

Gregor's brows lifted. "And he limped the entire way through the hospital just to say hello and then leave?"

"What are you saying?"

"Oh, I don't know." He angled his head and met my gaze. "What could I be saying?"

"If it's what I think, there's nothing going on between us. He's my friend."

"So you say."

"How dare you, when there's a photo of you with your wife out there for all to see!" I couldn't hold it any longer.

"So, you don't believe me?"

My eyes narrowed. "I don't think I do."

"If that's the way you think, I'm out of here."

I gulped. Why hadn't I stopped myself from saying that? I reached for him. "I'm sorry. I didn't mean it."

His eyes smouldered. "If that's true, come back to the hotel with me."

"Okay." My voice was small. Apologetic. Pathetic. I blew out a breath and grabbed my keys, but as I started to leave, I took a twenty-dollar bill from my purse and left it on the counter with a scribbled note and the Chinese restaurant number.

Later, when Gregor began undressing me, I tried to convince myself this is what I wanted, but I couldn't do it. I pulled away. I left him at the hotel and cried myself to sleep in my own bed.

EARLY THE NEXT morning my phone buzzed. I knew it would be Gregor. I reached over and picked it up.

I'm sorry, Kayla, I got called back. I'm at the airport. I'll call.

I threw my phone onto the floor. Words I'd never want my mother to hear flowed from my mouth. Deep down I'd known he didn't love me. Just because I wouldn't sleep with him, he'd left in a huff. I replied and told him not to bother. I tried to go back to sleep, but it was useless. I felt bereft and desolate. Besides, I needed to find out how my father was.

I climbed out of bed and stepped into the bathroom to take a shower. As the warm water spilled over my body, I decided that I didn't love Gregor DuBois anymore. Maybe I'd never loved him. Hot tears flowed down my cheeks, mingling with the shower water. I stayed in the shower longer than normal, shedding tears for what might have been. I needed more time to erase the nauseating grief of loss that gripped my heart, but it was the right thing to do. To let go of him. To move on. He didn't love me. The only person Gregor DuBois loved was himself.

After many long minutes, I turned the tap off, stepped out of the shower and dried myself slowly. As I looked in the mirror, I wondered where Kayla Mac had gone. Her fans wouldn't recognize her at the moment. I decided to go make-up free and let my skin breathe. I'd be plain Kayla McCormack until I returned. But my enthusiasm to return to that life was waning, which came as a shock because it *was* my life. I figured I just needed time to regroup after letting Gregor go.

I slipped on a simple dress, one I hadn't worn in many years but still hung in my closet. Mom would be surprised. Whenever she saw me, she always asked why I didn't wear dresses. Just another thing she didn't approve of. At least she couldn't nag me about Gregor anymore. I pushed back fresh tears. I wouldn't cry for him. He didn't deserve my tears.

I opened my door and walked through the house and into the kitchen. Mom wasn't there, but she called from the sitting room. "There's coffee in the pot, Kayla." Her voice sounded crisp, annoyed.

"Thanks." I poured myself a cup and sat on another chair opposite her. "I'm sorry about last night. I should have been home earlier."

"You're a grown woman, Kayla. You can do what you like."

That was a first. "I know."

"I saw the newspaper with the photo on the way home."

I cringed. "He's gone."

She lifted her gaze. "I'm glad. He wasn't right for you."

"I know. How's Dad?"

"He's doing well."

I smiled. "That's good. I'll go and see him this morning."

"He'll like that."

I swallowed hard. "I'm sorry for being horrible to you, Mom."

She looked up, her eyes widening before growing moist. She reached out her hand. "I've always just wanted the best for you, Kayla. It's grieved me to see you settling for less."

She was right. I thought I had it all, but apart from my music, my life was empty. "I know." I took her hand and squeezed it.

"What are you going to do?"

"I need to finish my tour. After that, I don't know."

"You'll always be welcome here."

"Thank you." I swallowed hard. It was nice to hear those words and feel for once they were genuine.

"I won't nag."

I quirked a brow and laughed. "You won't be you if you don't nag!"

"That's a nice thing to say." Mom sounded offended, but I knew she wasn't.

"I'll think about it." I doubted I could come back here to live. At least, not in this house, and maybe not even in Shelton. Not after living in a big city for so long, but the idea didn't seem as strange as it had just a few short days ago.

"Would you like some breakfast? I can make you something."

"I can look after myself. I'm a grown woman, remember?" I stood and walked to the kitchen.

"I know, but you'll always be my little girl."

"Don't get sentimental on me." I chuckled as I inspected the fridge.

"I'm not."

"I think you are."

She appeared in the kitchen behind me. "Maybe just a little. I've missed having you around."

I turned to face her. "I promise not to stay away as long in the future."

"Thank you, sweetheart. I know Dad would like that, too."

"I hope he makes it." I gulped. That horrid dream still haunted me.

"I think he will."

"That's not just God talk, is it?" I pulled a carton of juice from the fridge and poured a glass.

"No. The doctors are quietly confident."

"I still wish he'd come back to L.A. with me."

She rubbed my arm. "You know he won't."

"Yes, I know." I looked up as Adam joined us in the kitchen.

"What are you making, sis? Other than a mess."

I glared at him. "Nothing for you, that's for sure."

"No need to be rude."

"I'm not."

"Yes you are. Otherwise you would have offered to share."

"What? My juice?"

He shrugged. "Whatever."

I felt like throwing the juice into his face but stopped myself. Instead, I just glared at him. No, I could never come back to live here if Adam was around. We never did get along, always sparring like cats and dogs. Nothing had changed. "Gregor has left, before you say anything."

"Thank goodness for that. He was a slimy creature. I don't know what you saw in him."

And to be honest, neither did I.

SHORTLY AFTER, I drove Mom to the hospital. She wanted to stay all day with Dad, and I had no plans. I'd lost touch with all my old school friends. I assumed they'd all moved away, as I had. The only friend I now had was Dane, and I hardly remembered him from school days. Thinking of Dane made me think I could go and visit him again today. There was something fascinating about him. He lived such a simple life, yet he seemed so happy. And I quite enjoyed chatting with him and watching him work. Maybe he'd even let me have another turn on his wheel.

I walked into the hospital with Mom, feeling quite feminine in my dress. Dad was sitting up when we entered his room, but his eyes were closed. He must have heard us even though we tried to be quiet, because they fluttered then opened. His face lit up in one of his warm smiles. "Ah, my two most favorite women!"

I laughed and stepped forward, hugging him carefully. "Don't tell Jennifer that. Good to see you, Dad. You're looking well."

He winced as he adjusted his position. "And so are you." He winked at me.

I knew he was referring to my dress. He couldn't be talking about my face as it was so plain, although he'd often told me I wore too much make-up.

Mom stepped forward and kissed his cheek. The softness in the look that passed between them confirmed they were still deeply in love after almost thirty years of marriage. I doubted that if Gregor and I had been together that long we'd still be looking at each other like that. Would I ever find anyone I'd go the distance with? Most marriages in the entertainment industry lasted less than ten years; thirty was almost unheard of, so I somehow doubted it.

Mom and I sat and chatted with Dad for a while before he drifted off to sleep again. I decided I'd leave them alone for a while. Besides, Adam and Jennifer, and possibly a whole group of people from their church, would no doubt be in soon. I told Mom I'd come back for her later in the day.

"Okay, sweetheart. I won't ask where you're going."

I smiled. I almost told her, but I didn't want her reading too much into it.

16

DANE

FRIENDSHIP. *"A sweet friendship refreshens the soul."*

I WAS LIFTING a tray of pots and other items from the kiln when Kayla walked in. I almost dropped the entire tray on the floor. The last time I'd seen her in a dress was when she was ten years old. She looked so different... feminine, attractive. I swallowed hard and regained my composure. "Kayla! I didn't expect to see you today. Come in." I didn't say that I assumed she'd be with her boyfriend. My guess after a longer glance was that she'd been crying. Maybe they'd had a falling out. It wouldn't have surprised me after meeting him in person and then seeing that photo. She was short-selling herself by hanging around with him.

She smiled, thanked me, and followed me to the shelf where I was placing the tray. "Is one of them mine?"

"No, yours is still drying. It might go in next time."

"You did a good job fixing it."

I chuckled. "I've had lots of experience. How's your father?"

"He's doing well. I've just come from the hospital."

"That's good to hear. Would you like coffee?"

"Yes, please, but let me make it."

"Okay. I'll have one, too, and my mom made some cookies. They're in that container beside the coffee."

"I thought you'd have chocolate."

"And I thought you might have brought marshmallows." I chuckled again. It was such a strange relationship, but it worked.

"No. I need to lose weight before next week."

"You're definitely going back?"

"I have to." She heaped spoonsful of coffee into my old coffee maker and turned it on. "I'm sorry about yesterday."

"What do you mean?" I feigned ignorance, but I knew full well what she meant.

"About not telling you Gregor was coming."

"You didn't need to."

"No, but I should have. Anyway, he's gone."

I detected regret in her voice, but I was gladdened to hear this news. "Are you okay?"

She paused for a moment and then nodded. "He wasn't right for me."

"I didn't think so, either."

She grunted and grabbed two mugs from the shelf. "I don't want to stop you from working. I can sit and watch."

"It's okay. I needed a break."

"Thanks for coming to the hospital yesterday."

"I just wanted to pass on my best wishes."

"I know. But thank you." She handed me my coffee and

settled onto a stool. "I talked civilly with my mother this morning."

I smiled. "Good for you. And did she reply in kind?"

Her eyes brightened. "She did."

"That's progress."

"Yes. Why are you always so encouraging and positive?"

"I'm not."

"You are around me."

I wasn't sure how to respond. I didn't want to go spiritual on her, but the truth was that it was God at work that made me that way. My natural attitudes and thoughts weren't anywhere near as honorable. "You won't get annoyed if I'm honest with you?"

"Why would I?"

"Well, it's just that it's going to include some God talk, and I know you don't like it."

She sighed and shook her head. "I should have guessed as much. But go on."

"As long as you're sure."

"I'm sure." She rolled her eyes and then grinned.

I laughed. "Okay, then." I shared with her about the study I'd done with the boys at Boys' Club about the impurities in raw clay that often can't be seen, but that can have disastrous consequences if not removed. I then shared about how God wants His believers to live a holy life, and that He slowly but surely removes all the lumps and bumps from our lives, just like the boys and I did with the clay, so that it's smooth and clean.

"Since my suicide attempt and recommitting my life to God, I ask Him every day to show me areas of my life that need cleaning. He knows I've struggled with anger and negative thoughts, so that's one part of my life I focus on. I consciously choose to only think good thoughts. If a bad thought enters my mind, I refuse to let it take hold, and I replace it with a positive one. It's not always easy, but it's worthwhile. I know that it not only encourages those I meet, but it also helps me, especially on days when my leg is giving me pain."

She studied me for a while; I assume weighing up if I were nuts or for real. I hoped she'd decide I was for real, because I was. I was one hundred percent for real. I'd tasted life apart from God, and I knew it was empty and without purpose. It might look like fun, but the fun was short lived. What God offered was life with meaning and purpose. A way of life, a way of love, kindness, peace, and fulfillment. And He didn't say we couldn't have fun. Maybe I didn't have fun like she did, but I enjoyed my life, and I really did try to live the way God wanted me to. I hoped she could see that.

"Can't you do that without God?"

I chuckled. That was a good question. "Of course you can try, and some succeed, but since God offers His help, I'd be a fool to ignore that and try to do it on my own."

"What makes you so sure He's for real?"

"There's so much proof. Creation, for one. I know a lot of people refute that and say that it happened from a big bang and then everything evolved, and maybe there was a big bang, but there still had to be something that caused that in the first place. Nobody has ever made something out of nothing. Ever. And if you consider how intricate everything is, you'd need more faith to believe all of that happened by itself than to believe in an intelligent designer. And then there's the proof that Jesus actually existed, and that He didn't just die on the cross, but that He came back to life three days later."

She held up her hand. "Okay, that's enough."

I grimaced. "Sorry. I get carried away when I talk about this stuff."

"You don't say." Her tone was wry, but the sparkle in her eye suggested she was amused. "I can see you believe it. I guess it's better than not believing in something."

"I think so. Too many people these days have no idea what they believe in and just follow the latest fad without giving it any real thought."

"I can see you've given it lots."

"I have. Lots of study and reading. You can borrow some books if you want."

She shook her head, a horrified expression on her face. "I can't remember the last time I read a book."

"Maybe you could try. It's not as bad as you think."

"No, give me a movie any day."

"Sorry. I don't have any of those."

"We could go see one."

"What? You and me, go to the movies?"

"Why not?"

I blinked. I could give her several reasons, but as I thought them through, none held any weight. *I don't go to movies.* She'd say, *you can start now. What would people think if they saw us together?* She'd say, *does it matter? We probably wouldn't find one we'd both like.* She'd say, *let's try.* I drew a slow breath. "Okay. What do you want to see?"

Her face lit up. "Really? Are you serious?"

I shrugged. "I guess so. It's not something I'd normally do, but why not? As long as Gregor isn't in it."

"Agreed. You probably wouldn't like his movies, anyway."

"When do you want to go?"

"Whenever suits you."

"Tonight?"

"Sounds perfect. Tonight it is."

"I'll pick you up at seven."

She smiled. "I'll look forward to it."

"Now I'd better get back to work."

"Mind if I watch for a while? I promise I won't distract you."

I could have said I didn't mind if she did, but I replied that it was fine, I could work and talk at the same time. Although talking with Kayla would always be distracting. How could it not? My mother was right. I still had a crush on her, and now we were going to the movies. But we were going as friends. We could be nothing more than that unless she decided to follow Jesus. It was wrong to be unequally yoked, and as much as I liked her, I would not even consider going down that path, even now that she was single again. And I certainly would not pressure her to follow Jesus just so we could be more than friends. Not that I expected she would do that for a second, or even that she wanted to be more than friends.

For the next hour or so, Kayla watched me work. We chatted easily, which was a pleasant surprise. I'd never chatted easily with a girl before. I asked her about her concerts and what she liked about singing and performing so much. I asked her about L.A. and where she lived. She asked me about my family and if I'd lived anywhere other than Shelton. I surprised her by saying that other than my short stay in the Marines, I'd always lived here. Some people would say I'd lived a sheltered life. Maybe I had, and maybe that was why when I did leave, I didn't know how to handle my freedom. Now I was older, I was content to be here with my work and my church and my

Boys' Club, but if God asked me to move, I would gladly do so. He just hadn't asked.

Finally. she said she needed to go. "I told Mom I'd go back for her. I'll look forward to tonight."

I smiled and said I would too. "We still haven't decided what to watch."

"I'll see what's on."

"Okay. I'll trust you."

She chuckled. "Are you sure you want to do that?"

"I don't know. But I will."

"You're so sweet." She surprised me by stepping close and kissing my cheek before she bounced away.

I was dumbfounded. Why would she have done that? I released a sigh. I hoped she wasn't replacing Gregor DuBois with me, like a rebound thing. She'd get hurt again if she was. I spent the next few minutes praying for her, and for me. That small kiss had changed our relationship whether she knew it or not, and neither of us were prepared for that. I was happier when we were just friends, pre-kiss—although I lifted my hand to the place where her lips had touched, and smiled.

17

KAYLA

REALITY. *"If we claim to be without sin, we deceive ourselves and the truth is not in us."*

I COULDN'T WIPE the smile off my face as I left Dane's workshop. He was the most unlikely person for me to fall for, but after Gregor's shallowness, Dane's depth of character inspired me to be a better person. I doubted I'd ever read a book, but I *would* start giving thought to what I believed in. What he'd said made sense, but I wasn't ready to jump in and change my life just yet. Maybe I never would be, but I'd give it some serious attention.

Having been raised in a family that believed in and followed God, I knew all the Bible stories, although I'd never fully understood them. And I'd sung in the church choir, so I knew the old hymns, but the words had never come alive for me. But listening to Dane made me think that maybe God was actually real and alive. He certainly believed it, and he lived it.

I'd never met anyone who took his commitment so seriously. No, on second thought, my parents did, but that was different. They were my parents. Since when did a child heed his or her parents? I knew children should, but my mother in particular hadn't been as loving and kind to me as I expected a Christian mother should be. Maybe I was being the judgmental one now, but it was true. I'd never felt that she loved me unconditionally. All I felt was her judgment.

Pulling into the hospital parking lot, I realized I needed to change my thoughts towards my mother. Dane's words came back to me... *If a bad thought enters my mind, I refuse to let it take hold and I replace it with a positive one.* Okay, I'll replace that negative thinking with positive thoughts. I know my mother loves me and only wants the best for me. She told me so this morning. We'd hopefully turned a corner in our relationship, and she seemed to be prepared to meet me halfway. Now, how hard was that? I didn't need God in my life to do that.

I parked the car and walked quickly to Dad's room. A number of people I didn't know stood around his bed. I couldn't see Mom, Adam or Jennifer anywhere. I backed out of the room without being noticed. It helped that they were all praying for him and had their eyes closed, but I bumped into someone and turned around. I almost knocked her over... I knew who she was immediately. The nosy woman from church. She looked old when I was a kid. She looked even older now. Her arms flew up as she grabbed for something to stop her from teetering over. I had to help her since I couldn't let her fall. "I'm sorry, Mrs. Steward. I didn't see you there."

"It's okay. You don't have eyes in the back of your head." *No, but you do...* I almost burst out laughing. If only she knew what I was thinking. She glanced around me. "No boyfriend?"

"No, no boyfriend."

"Oh. That was a quick visit."

"Yes, he had to go back for work." I could see she was itching to ask me something more. She'd probably seen the photo, but I wasn't going to give her any space to even mention it. "Are you visiting my father?"

"Yes, yes. And I'm late. I can see all the others are already in there."

"I'll let you get on then. Sorry for bumping into you."

"It's quite all right, dear. No harm done."

"Thank you." I bid her goodbye and escaped. Mom had to be somewhere. The cafeteria? I headed that way and found her, Adam and Jennifer sitting at a table eating sandwiches. She waved me over, so I joined them.

"Have you had lunch, sweetheart?"

"No, but I'm not hungry." I didn't say I needed to lose weight before I returned to work. Mom would tell me that was nonsense; I needed to put it on, not take it off. But I knew what Lawrence would say.

She handed me half of hers. "Take it, Kayla. You need to eat."

I let out a resigned sigh. "Okay. Thank you." Egg and lettuce wasn't my favorite sandwich filling, but I'd eat it just to keep Mom happy. I took a nibble and then asked how Dad was.

"He's been sleeping a lot."

"Well, he's not now. He couldn't with all those people around him."

"They've just come to pray for him. They won't be there long."

"Good. There were way too many. I'm surprised they were allowed in at the same time."

"Reverend Matthew spoke to the head nurse. She said it was okay."

"Reverend Matthew gets preferential treatment?"

"Kayla, stop it!" Jennifer burst out. "You should hear yourself."

I blew out an annoyed breath. I hadn't meant to speak like that. I don't know what happened. Maybe it was bumping into that nosy woman, or seeing all the people around *my* father, but my resolution to speak nicely to my mother hadn't even made it to first base. "I'm sorry," I said as meekly as I could.

Mom placed her hand on my wrist. "It's okay, sweetheart. I know you've got a lot to deal with."

I raised my brow. That was a first. Mom had never acknowledged how hard I worked. As much as I loved performing, it *was* hard work. But I felt she was actually referring to my break-up with Gregor. She must have assumed I was struggling with it, and she would have been right, until I visited Dane. Just the thought of him made me smile. I don't know what had made me kiss him. I hadn't meant to; it just happened. I hoped I hadn't embarrassed him. "Yes, but I shouldn't have spoken like that."

I saw the look that passed between Adam and Jennifer and chuckled to myself. They didn't know that the new Kayla had arrived in town. *The nice one,* thanks to Dane Carmichael.

Ten minutes later we returned to Dad's bedside. The church folk had left, but he looked tired. He needed rest, so we kissed him and gave him a hug and then left, promising to return later.

Mom came back home with me, while Adam dropped Jennifer at her house. Mom had suggested she come back with us for the afternoon, but she said she had things that needed doing. I wasn't convinced. I was sure she bowed out because she didn't want to spend time with me. I shrugged it off. I wasn't too eager to spend time with her, either.

I knew Mom was itching to ask where I'd gone earlier on. I didn't offer the information, and she didn't ask, although I think it almost killed her. I also didn't tell her about going to the movies with Dane that evening, although she'd find out when he picked me up. I'd deal with that then.

I spent the rest of the afternoon catching up on my work emails and preparing as much as I could for my performances the following week. The only guitar I had at home was an old one, but it was good enough for me to run through my songs, although I couldn't belt them out like I'd do on stage or at rehearsal. The more I sang, the more my enthusiasm returned, and by the time Dane picked me up, I was wondering why I'd even been thinking I could give it up.

I kept an eye out for his pickup. I still hadn't told Mom who I was going to the movies with, only that I was going. I didn't want her to read more into it than there was. As he pulled up outside our house, I called out that my ride was here. She was in the kitchen so she called out for me to have a good time. I was in the clear. I opened the door quickly, closed it behind me, and then ran down the steps and jumped into the passenger seat. Dane had already opened the door from the inside. I don't know that I'd expected him to open the door for me like a gentleman, but I was slightly disappointed he hadn't, although relieved at the same time. It would have slowed our take-off and given Mom more time to see who I was going with. I should have told him I'd meet him in town, but it was kind of nice having him pick me up.

I smiled and thanked him. He'd changed into fresh clothes

and wore cologne. He'd also combed his hair a little differently. He looked nice. I'd changed out of my dress and was wearing a pair of skinny black jeans, a slinky shirt and boots. I'd also applied a little mascara and lip gloss. I didn't feel comfortable going completely bare-faced, but it was still less make-up than I usually wore.

"What movie did you choose?"

"The Greatest Showman. Have you heard of it?"

He glanced at me. "I don't go to the movies, remember?"

"Yes, I remember. I think you'll like it, although it's a musical."

"Really?"

"Not my type of music, but it was hard to find something I thought we'd both like."

He chuckled as he slowed to take a corner. "Okay, I'll believe you." He turned his head, and as our gazes met, I laughed at the amused grin on his face.

After we parked, I was tempted to hold his hand but thought better of it. I'd already over-stepped the mark by kissing him. He paid for our tickets, which I thought was neat, considering I earned a lot more than he did. Well, I assumed I did. I couldn't imagine he'd make that much selling pottery. We also bought popcorn and ice creams. I forgot that I was supposed to be losing weight.

The theatre was in semi-darkness when we entered. I led the way and found our seats which were towards the back. We settled in and I smiled when he asked if it was usual for the theatre to be full. "It depends on the movie, but it's what most normal people do to relax."

He leaned closer and whispered in my ear, "Are you saying I'm not normal?"

"Maybe." Dane Carmichael was anything but normal.

We both enjoyed the movie. I was relieved. I was also thankful that there was very little bad language in it. I didn't think Dane would have coped if there had been a lot, being Mr. Squeaky Clean.

As we filed out of the theatre, the crush of people pushed us together. He put his arm around my shoulder, more to protect me than anything I assumed, but it felt nice. I snuggled closer and wondered what it would be like to have him hold me properly. To have him kiss me. I stopped myself at that point; I'd already gone too far.

Dane dropped his arm as we left the crush. I was disappointed, but I'd let my imagination run wild and shouldn't have. We were just friends, although I was beginning to think I wanted more. "Would you like to get something before we go?"

"Like what?"

"I don't know. I'm not used to doing this."

"Coffee?"

"Okay. Do you know a place?"

"There's only one place that I know of that would be open."

"The Roadhouse?"

I nodded. "The Roadhouse."

Dane shook his head. "Let's give it a miss. I don't want to be in tomorrow's headlines."

I chuckled. "Neither do I. Why don't we go to your place?"

He looked taken aback. "I don't think that's a good idea."

"What, then?"

"Maybe I should just drop you home. I've got to be at church early tomorrow."

My shoulders sagged. I didn't want the night to end. To go home to my parents' home alone. Mom would probably be in bed and if he were home, Adam would only give me a hard time. "Can't we go somewhere and talk?"

"I'd love to, but I really do need to be up early. Why don't you come with me?"

My head jerked up. "To church?"

"Yes. Why not?"

He had me over a barrel, although going to the movies was nothing like going to church. I let out a resigned sigh and reluctantly agreed.

"Great. I need to be there early, but I can pick you up about eight-fifty. Or you could get a lift with your mother."

I shuddered. What would Mom say when I told her I was going to church? No doubt she'd be over-the-moon and gush all over me. I didn't want that. I was only going because Dane had agreed to go to the movies with me. But he was right; I should go with her. She'd be disappointed if I didn't. I agreed.

He smiled and started the car and headed in the direction of my folks' home. I sat quietly, wondering how he'd gotten me to agree. I could still change my mind.

When he pulled up outside our house, I half hoped he'd lean across and kiss me. He didn't, but he did give me a smile that was almost as intimate. "I enjoyed tonight, Kayla. Thanks for suggesting it."

I fought to control my overwhelming desire to be close to him. "You're welcome. Maybe we can do it again some time."

"Next time you're back in town?"

I smiled broadly. "It's a deal." I broke my resolve and popped another kiss on his cheek and jumped out before I did something more I'd regret.

Dane shook his head and laughed. "See you in the morning."

I gave a backwards wave and ran lightly up the front steps, turning to see his taillights disappear around the corner. I was falling for Dane Carmichael, but it was foolishness. He was too nice for the likes of me. I was Kayla Mac, and my life was in L.A. I had to leave before it was too late.

18

DANE

DISAPPOINTMENT. *"Why are you cast down, O my soul, and why are you in turmoil within me?*

WHEN MARIANNE MCCORMACK walked into church without Kayla, disappointment sagged through me. I'd so hoped she'd come, but I guess I should have expected her not to. With so much antagonism towards God and church, to think she'd come on my first invitation was unrealistic. God could still work in her heart, however, whether she was in church or not. I prayed that He would.

I loved being in church, singing songs of praise, worshiping my Father. I could never have enough of it. As I took my seat in the pew beside my mother and father, I thought of all the amazing things God kept doing in my life, things I didn't deserve. I thought of all I had, things I didn't ask for and couldn't even work for. My mother told me once that God loved me as if I was the only person on earth, that He loved every single person in that same way. He was capable of such wondrous things, and much more beyond my comprehension. That kind of love and consistency in His promises would never cease to amaze me. If only Kayla could understand that. As soon as church finished I checked my phone and smiled when I saw she'd sent a message. My smile slipped when I read it.

I'm sorry I didn't come to church. I couldn't. My life is too much of a mess. I'm going back to L.A. today. Thanks for last night, I enjoyed it. Kayla.

Going back today? Without even saying goodbye? I was shocked. Disappointed. I quickly typed a reply.

Can I see you before you go?

Her reply was instant. *I'm at the hospital with Dad and then I'm going to the airport. You can meet there if you want, but it's okay if you don't.*

I typed back, *I'll be there.*

I quickly did my rounds of the boys as I did every Sunday, but my mind and heart were on someone else. As soon as I could, I left and drove to the airport. Being such a small town, the airport was also small, and I couldn't miss her. I scanned the outside area but couldn't see her. I went inside; she wasn't there either. Not unexpected; she was no doubt still with her father.

The airport didn't have a coffee shop, just a vending machine. I took out my coins and popped them into the machine and selected a cappuccino. Not that I wanted one, but it would pass the time while I waited for Kayla.

Finally, her car pulled into the rental returns area. While I'd been waiting, more people had arrived and as she wheeled her suitcase inside, she almost blended in. But not quite. Heads turned and stared at her. Even with her brown hair, she was still recognizable as Kayla Mac.

I waved to her awkwardly and walked as fast as I could to greet her. I was very conscious of my leg and tried not to limp. A futile exercise. I forgot about it as our gazes met. Gone was the happy, carefree Kayla who'd sat beside me last night at the movies, who'd leaned in close when I put my arm around her, who'd popped a kiss on my cheek when I dropped her home. This Kayla wore a sad, heavy demeanor. Something was going on inside her. I sensed it was a spiritual battle and she was running away.

I didn't smile at her. How could I when she was leaving? Unfamiliar feelings squeezed my heart. I stepped closer and hugged her. She rested her head against my chest. I drew her close and held her; she felt like a small child who needed comforting.

We remained that way for what seemed forever. Finally she pulled away. Her face was damp, so I handed her a tissue. She blew her nose and composed herself. "I'm sorry." Her voice was tiny, as if she were about to burst into tears. For her sake, I didn't want that to happen in public and run the risk of it being splashed over tomorrow's paper. Not that any newspaper reporters frequented the Shelton airport.

I directed her to a row of seats away from the crowd and we sat. I looked at her and prayed that God would help me out. I was out of my depth. "Kayla, what happened?"

She shrugged and dabbed her eyes. I sensed she couldn't speak.

"It's okay. I think I know what's going on. You're like one of my pots that's just gone into the kiln. The heat's been turned up and you're feeling uncomfortable." I didn't tell her it could get hotter. "Your life might be a mess, but God loves fixing messes. Give Him a chance." I handed her a Bible I'd picked up from church. "Take this. I know you don't read books, but please read this one. It will change your life." I prayed that she'd take it, and my heart warmed when she did.

"I'm sorry, Dane. I've let you down."

"No, you haven't. Going to church is important, but what's going on inside you is even more so. I'll be praying for you, okay? And please stay in touch, will you?"

She nodded. That was all I could ask for. Even if we were miles apart, at least if we were talking I could support her through the tough times. "We can skype."

"Skype?"

She rolled her red, watery eyes. "Don't tell me you've never skyped?"

"I can't say that I have, sorry."

"Show me your phone."

She scrolled through my apps and stopped at one I'd not noticed and held it closer to me. "See that big S?"

I nodded.

"That's skype. I'll send you a friend request and if you click on it, we can talk and see each other at the same time."

My brows lifted. "I've heard of it but never had need to use it before."

She chuckled. "You can now."

It was good she was talking again. It wasn't good that her flight had just been called.

I studied her delicate face, fine like porcelain. I wanted to take in her every detail. I didn't have a photo of her, but her image would be etched on my mind. I couldn't have her, but I loved her. That realization struck me in the chest like a bolt of lightning.

"I need to go." She looked into my eyes.

I gulped. "I know."

"I'll miss you."

"Not as much as I'll miss you." I took a deep breath. I wasn't used to this kind of talk with a girl.

She gave me a winsome smile. "Thank you."

"What for?"

"For being my friend."

I pulled her close and hugged her, while fighting the urge to kiss her and ask her to stay. "Take care."

She sucked in a big breath and her body shuddered. "I'll try."

We stood and I walked with her to the gate and gave her another hug. She kissed my cheek and then she smiled and walked away.

An inexplicable sense of loneliness washed over me. I'd never had a friend like her before, and now she was gone. I limped slowly back to my pickup, but instead of climbing in, I leaned against it and watched her plane take off. I prayed that whatever lay ahead of her, God would be with her, drawing her softly and gently to Himself, and that maybe one day He'd bring her back home, to me.

19

KAYLA

TRUTH. *"In the beginning was the Word..."*

I HUNKERED down in my seat and closed my eyes. Somewhere below, Dane would be driving home in his pickup. To his workshop; to his pots. On the other hand, the glitz and glamor of L.A. awaited me. It was what I wanted. It was my life.

If that were true, why did I feel so rotten? Like I'd just walked away from my best friend after slapping him in the face?

I let out a heavy sigh and stared out the window. Dad hadn't wanted me to leave and made me promise to come back soon. I gave him that promise, but wondered if I could keep it. Could I face my family again after walking out on them? No doubt Mom would be livid when she read my note. Adam would say it was typical. Jennifer wouldn't care.

Dad and Dane. They'd be who I'd return for. But would I? Lawrence had all of my concerts lined up, plus a meeting with a production company. He was so excited about the prospect of doing a television series. I couldn't share his enthusiasm but knew it would help fill my void.

I closed my eyes and tried to sleep, but thoughts of Dane filled my mind. As simple as he was, he'd captured my heart, but I couldn't share his faith. I'd done too many bad things in my life… killed my baby, slept with so many men I'd lost count, drank, smoked and swore. Who would want me with that list? Neither Dane nor his God. I may as well forget about him and throw myself into my work. My music. It's what made me happiest.

I dozed on and off for a few hours, disturbed only by a flight attendant asking if I'd like a refreshment. I shook my head and pulled my cap over my face. The seat beside me was empty, so I'd escaped the need for small talk.

Finally, the plane began its descent into L.A. The lights of the city spread as far as the eye could see. I straightened and stretched, remembering one of the reasons I rarely went home. A ten-hour flight did absolutely nothing for me.

I hadn't told Lawrence I was coming home a day early, so he wasn't there to meet me. I grabbed my luggage and hailed a cab. I lived in an apartment in Westwood, but I was rarely there because of my touring agenda; I spent most of my time in hotels that could have been anywhere. I had one day. One day to do whatever I wanted. But first I wanted a hot tub, a bottle of red wine and a good sleep.

The cab ride took half an hour. Even on a Sunday evening, traffic was chaotic. Horns blasted and drivers gestured rudely at each other. So different from Shelton where most folks were polite and rarely a horn was blown. But this was L.A., the City of Angels, so there was no comparison.

My apartment took up the whole of the twenty-third floor.

My parents had no idea how much it had cost, and I'd never tell them. As I opened the door, I wanted it to feel like home, but although it was chic and modern, it was cold, clinical and empty. I turned my music on and blasted it through every speaker. Normally that did the trick, but within minutes I turned it down. I loved my songs, but right now all I wanted was sleep. I ran my bath and checked messages while I chose a bottle of wine. My mother had left three voice messages, all much the same.

Why did you leave without saying goodbye? I don't understand.

Call when you get in. Please.

I thought we were getting on better.

I'd call her tomorrow. I couldn't handle it tonight.

Climbing into the hot tub reminded me of the words Dane had spoken to me just that morning. I didn't want to remember them, but he was right. I hadn't gone to church because the heat had been turned up on my life, exposing all my hidden cracks. Now I wanted to forget his words and cover those cracks. Wine would do that. I poured a glass, and as I sipped, I let the warm water flow around my body. Bliss. Pure, unadulterated bliss.

I stayed there until my skin looked like a bunch of prunes. I climbed out, dried myself and slipped into my fluffy pink robe. Grabbing my wine and a packet of marshmallows, I headed straight for my king-size bed, but poking out of my suitcase was the Bible Dane had given me that morning. I tried to ignore it, but it was like an itch that needed scratching. I let out an annoyed sigh and tucked it under my arm, but as I climbed onto the bed, a piece of paper slipped out. I adjusted my pillows and cushions and then opened it. My eyes widened. It was a handwritten note from Dane, addressed to me.

Dear Kayla,

I don't know when you'll read this, or even if you will, because you might never open this Bible. But if you're reading it, it means you have, and that gladdens me.

I really appreciated the short time we spent together. We're so different, but I feel we've started a friendship that will last the distance. I know that the thought of going to church scared you off. It doesn't matter. God loves you and He'll keep reminding you of that in so many different ways until you believe it for yourself. He's a loving Father who only wants the best for you, but He won't force you to return His love. It's your choice, but I pray that one day you'll grasp how wide, how long, how high, and how deep His love for you is.

You're a unique creation, like the pot you made that's sitting on the shelf waiting to be fired. There's no one like you, Kayla McCormack. It doesn't matter what's in your past, God will forgive you, if only you ask. My greatest joy would be to welcome you into the family of Christ, but until then, I'm happy to be your friend.

Please stay in touch and call me whenever you'd like to chat.

Your friend,

Dane Carmichael

I wiped tears from my eyes. Trust Dane to have that effect on me, even when we were miles apart. I re-read the letter and then opened the Bible. I had no idea where to start, but I vaguely remembered from Sunday School days that the book of John was a good place. I looked in the index, found it and began reading. *"In the beginning was the Word, and the Word was with God, and the Word was God. He was with God in the beginning. Through him all things were made; without him nothing was made that has been made. In him was life, and that life was the light of all mankind."*

I didn't fully understand it, but something moved deep

inside me. I wanted to know more; I wanted to know about the life that was the light of all mankind. I grabbed my laptop and opened Skype. Dane wouldn't know what to do, so I sent him a message with instructions, and then punched in his number.

His face appeared on my phone screen and I smiled. "Hey nerd, you got it working."

"Watch it. Two can play at that game."

I laughed, but then grew serious. "I read it."

"The note?"

I nodded and bit my lip.

"And?"

"Thank you."

Dane's voice was soft. "What for?"

"For being my friend." My voice wavered as unexpected emotion grabbed me.

"So you opened it?"

"The Bible?"

It was his turn to nod. "Yes."

"I did."

"Did you read any of it?"

"A few verses."

"That's a good start."

"I didn't understand it. It's been a long time since I was in Sunday school or tried to learn anything except new lyrics. I'm out of practice."

He smiled. "That's okay. Ask God to show you what it means as you read. And we can talk about it if you want."

"Thanks. I'll see how it goes."

We looked at each other for a few seconds before he asked how my flight was.

I rolled my eyes and sighed. "Long."

"Have you called your mother?"

I shook my head and grimaced. "Not yet."

"I heard she's not happy."

I frowned. "How did you hear that?"

"Need you ask?"

I groaned. "No. I'll call her in the morning."

We shared a comfortable silence for a few moments before Dane spoke. "I miss you already."

I brushed tears from my eyes. "And me, you."

"When do you start work?"

"Tuesday." I sniffed.

"What will you do tomorrow?"

"I don't know. Sleep, probably."

"Well, take care. Call me whenever you want." His voice was soft. Gentle. Caring.

I swallowed hard. "I will."

"Good night."

I smiled and blew him a kiss before I ended the call.

Leaning back against my pillows, I wondered if we'd ever move past this friendship. I was pulled in two directions—the life I knew and loved; it was the one that offered excitement, fame and fortune. And then there was the simple life; the one with the love of God and Dane, because I sensed that he did love me, although he'd never said it. And I knew deep down that God also loved me. I'd just never been prepared to give up what I thought was the life I wanted for the life I needed.

I sucked in a deep breath, and for the first time in a long time, possibly ever, I closed my eyes and prayed. My chest felt constricted and I thought I might cry. I didn't know what to say, so I just started. "God, if You exist, please reveal Yourself to me. Help me to understand and teach me Your ways. That is, if You're prepared to look past all the things I've done wrong in my life. I won't blame You if You don't."

I didn't know what to expect, but my heart felt lighter. I knew this was the beginning, like Dane had told me, but there always had to be a beginning, and this was mine.

Instead of drinking my wine, I turned the light off, slid down in the bed, tucked the bedcovers under my chin, and fell asleep.

20

DANE

ANGUISH. *"I am worn out calling for help; my throat is parched."*

I WOKE SOMETIME during the night to my phone buzzing. My immediate thought was that it was Kayla, but when I picked it up, I saw it was Reverend Matthew. I blinked and answered, dreading whatever news he was about to give. My gut told me it was nothing good.

"I'm sorry to wake you, Dane."

"It's okay. What's wrong?"

"It's Ivan."

My heart stopped. "What's happened?" I didn't want to ask, but I had to. I expected the worst.

"He tried to kill himself."

Blood drained from my face. "No…"

"I'm afraid so. Fortunately he didn't succeed, but he's critical."

"Where is he?"

"In the hospital. I thought you might want to come in."

"I do. I'll come right away."

I ended the call and quickly dressed before grabbing my keys and jumping into my pickup. I felt bad. I should have checked on him more often. I'd been so absorbed with Kayla I hadn't noticed he wasn't in church. In fact, I hadn't seen him since the day I'd dropped him at the corner of his street. Maybe I could have prevented this from happening if I hadn't been distracted and had paid him more attention. *I'm sorry, God. Please forgive me. Please help Ivan make it.* Ivan couldn't die, not when he had his whole life ahead of him. God had a purpose for his life. It couldn't end this way.

As it was the middle of the night when I arrived at the hospital, I had to wait in the waiting room for news, along with Reverend Matthew and Ivan's mother. I didn't think I'd met her before, but she looked vaguely familiar. Maybe I'd seen her at church. She looked too young to be his mom, and I guessed Ivan might not have been planned. If that was the case, and Ivan never knew his father, like he'd told me, it was possible she'd raised him on her own, possibly without any family support. I didn't know that, but it was a good guess. My heart went out to her. She must have had a tough time. And now he'd tried to kill himself. How terrible for her.

I tried to think why he would have done it. I knew from first-hand experience he would have felt he had no option; that he had no reason to live. That he'd lost hope. I'd failed him. I really thought we were making progress. Obviously, I was wrong. It made me wonder about all the other boys. Was I failing them, too? Did I really know what was going on in their lives, or was I just ticking the boxes with them and assuming they'd be okay? I didn't think so, but it did make me stop and think. I genuinely cared for those boys, including Ivan. I hoped they knew that. I didn't understand why Ivan hadn't spoken to me if he was feeling so desperate. Once again, I felt I'd failed because of my distraction with Kayla.

Reverend Matthew suggested we pray for Ivan. We bowed our heads and beseeched God to keep him alive, and for skill and wisdom for the doctors as they treated him. Reverend Matthew had told me Ivan had cut his wrists and had lost a lot of blood. I'd never considered that option; I'd tried to drown myself as I'd heard that was the least painful way. But praise God I was found in time and survived. I prayed Ivan would too.

We waited for some time, and finally a doctor, whom we all knew as he also attended the same church, told us that Ivan would survive. He was in recovery and we could see him for a few minutes shortly. We all breathed a sigh of relief and gave thanks to God, but we knew this was just the start of his recovery. The cause needed to be addressed, and ongoing counseling would be needed to ensure his mental health was such that it wouldn't happen again. I knew the drill. But even more than that, Ivan needed to truly know the God who created him and loved him deeply.

When we were allowed to see him, Reverend Matthew and I stood back to allow his mother to speak with him first. I could tell by the softness in her voice that she truly loved him. That was a good thing. When it was my turn to have a few words, I apologized. He said it wasn't my fault, and that he should have spoken with me that day I'd dropped him off. I learned later that his stepfather had been beating and abusing him. No wonder he'd felt desperate, but for now, I just assured him of my ongoing support.

Later, back at home, I had trouble falling asleep again, so I went into my workshop and began throwing another pot. As I did, I prayed for both Ivan and Kayla, that they both might come to know the true Potter, the One who had a wonderful plan for their lives and loved them so much that He sent His only Son to die so that they could have eternal life, be forgiven of their sin, and experience new and abundant life here on earth with meaning and purpose.

21

KAYLA

PURPOSE. *"Many are the plans in a person's heart, but it is the LORD's purpose that prevails."*

I SLEPT UNTIL MIDDAY. The persistent ringing of the door buzzer woke me. I dragged myself out of bed, slipped on my pink robe, and checked the monitor to see who it was. I groaned. What was Lawrence doing here? How did he even know I was home? Did the man have spies? Probably. I sighed and let him in.

Within moments, my quiet day had ended before it begun. He bounded in and gave me an air hug and kiss, and then stepped back, his eyes wide. "What *have* you done to your hair?"

I reached up and felt it, and then remembered I'd dyed it brown before I left to go home. "This is my natural color."

"Well, I don't like it, and neither will your fans. I'll make an appointment for you this afternoon."

He was at it already. "Can't it wait until tomorrow?"

"No, I've scheduled the meeting with the producers for nine a.m. You'll need to have it done today."

I walked to the kitchen and switched on the coffee machine. "Guess you'd like one?"

"Of course."

I sighed heavily. I didn't want to do this any longer, but how could I tell him?

"What happened with Gregor? I thought you two were a match made in heaven." He pulled up a stool and sat, watching my every move.

"He was seeing his wife."

His brow shot up. "So the papers were right?"

"I believe so." I grabbed two mugs from the shelf.

"Not your knight in shining armor, then?" He chuckled.

"Seems that way."

He grew serious. "Are you okay?"

I shrugged. I'd almost forgotten about Gregor, to be honest. Which was strange, as until a few days ago I'd planned to marry the jerk. "I'm over him."

"That was quick."

I nodded. "He wasn't right for me."

It seemed Lawrence didn't know what to say, because he remained quiet for a few moments before asking how my father was.

"He's stable. The surgeons think they got all the cancer. He starts radiation this week."

"He won't come here?"

"Nope." I dropped three lumps of sugar into Lawrence's coffee and passed it to him.

"You seem different. It's not just your hair. Is something wrong?"

"Apart from you interrupting my day, you mean?"

"Aw, come on Kayla. Don't be like that. Aren't you glad to see me?"

I thought for a moment and then broke into a smile. I couldn't remain upset with him for long. "Yes, Lawrence, I'm glad to see you, but don't hassle me, okay?"

"I don't hassle you."

"Yes, you do."

"Isn't that what you pay me to do? We're a team, Kayla. You do all the upfront and creative stuff, and I get the gigs."

"Yes, but don't hassle me today, please." I flopped onto the sofa.

"But you need to get your hair done. You can't go to the meeting like that."

"Change the meeting."

"No. They want to meet with you immediately."

"What if I don't want to meet with them at all?" I held his gaze.

His face paled. "You wouldn't do that, would you?"

As I toyed with my coffee mug, Dane's image flitted through my mind. These mugs were so boring compared to the ones he made. I needed to answer Lawrence. I should tell him, but he'd be devastated. Maybe I could see what they were offering. Keep him happy for a little longer.

I shrugged. "I've been thinking about it, but..."

"But what?" The desperation in his eyes made me wonder why it meant so much to him. I was his meal-ticket, but he was a good manager. He'd have no trouble getting another job.

"I'll go."

He let out a relieved breath. "You had me worried for a minute."

"You'd better book me that salon appointment," I said without any enthusiasm.

He whipped his phone out. "Onto it."

While he made the call, I glanced at my phone and remembered I needed to call Mom. But not in front of Lawrence. Later. I smiled when I saw a message from Dane. I must have been in a deep sleep since I hadn't heard my phone beep. I opened it and my eyes nearly fell out of my head. *Bad news... one of my boys tried to kill himself last night—the one you met in my shop. He didn't succeed, but he's a mess. I let him down. I feel so bad. Skype me tonight? Thinking of you. Dane*

I was stunned. For one, that this had happened. And two, that Dane had shared it with me. And not only that, he'd shared how he was feeling. His life was so real. Mine, it was so fake. I had no interest in starring in a television series that promoted fake, especially after this. I wasn't doing anything to help the world. My songs were about nothing that mattered. They were rubbish. I didn't know if I could even sing them anymore. But I'd have to. Lawrence had re-booked all the concerts. I couldn't cancel again. But my heart wouldn't be in them.

"Okay, two o'clock. They squeezed you in." His head tilted. "What's the matter? You look like you've seen a ghost."

"I just got some bad news."

"Not your father?"

I shook my head. "No, a kid back home tried to take his life."

"Oh, I'm sorry. Is he okay?"

I nodded. I was still trying to absorb the news.

"That's good. Lots of kids succeed."

"I know. It's sad."

"And that's why you need to grasp this opportunity, Kayla. You cheer them when you sing."

I knew I did. They loved me, but my songs meant nothing. My fans just liked the loud music. I didn't give them a reason to live. "I can't do this, Lawrence. I'll do my concerts, and then I'm taking an extended break."

"You're joking, right?"

"No, I'm serious."

"Is it the kid?"

I shook my head slowly.

"What, then? I don't understand."

I shrugged apologetically. "It's complicated."

"Try me."

"I don't understand it myself, so I doubt I could make you understand."

His forehead puckered as he slipped onto the sofa beside me. "I don't get it. You've got the world at your fingertips, and you're going to throw it away?" A muscle in his jaw twitched. I was scaring him.

"I'll take a break and see how I feel after that, okay?"

"You've just had a break."

"Yes, but it was only a week or so."

"It seemed like a year." He sounded so downcast.

I shrugged dismissively. I wouldn't do something I didn't want to do just to make him feel better. "You need to cancel the meeting."

"They won't be happy."

"Tell them I'm sorry."

He held my gaze. "You won't get another chance."

"I don't mind."

"You might."

I shook my head. "I don't think so. I'll get my hair done tomorrow. I need some time alone today."

His eyes widened. I'd offended him, but I didn't care. "You want me to go?"

"If you don't mind."

He stood and raked his hand through his hair. "I don't get it. I really don't get it. Take today off, but reconsider the meeting. Please."

"You'd let me go with brown hair?"

"I'd let you go with whatever color you want, so long as you go."

"I won't change my mind." We stared at each other like two bulls in the ring. I'd never been so certain of anything. I did not want to do this.

He began pacing. "You'll regret this, Kayla. You need to rethink."

"I'll be at rehearsal tomorrow after I've had my hair done. You'd best change that appointment."

"Change it yourself." And with that, he stormed out.

I RELEASED a huge breath and leaned against the back of the sofa. Had I done the right thing? My chest heaved. I hadn't thought about taking a break, but it made sense. Finish my tour and take a break. I could cite personal reasons. I didn't need to explain myself, although there'd be questions. There always were. I'd give Lawrence a good payout. He'd survive.

With that sorted, I called my mom. She answered on the first ring. "Kayla. Why did you leave without saying goodbye?"

"I shouldn't have. I'm sorry. I just got a little mixed up, that's all."

Silence. She hadn't expected that. "Are you all right?"

"I'm getting there." I sighed heavily. I hoped that was true.

"You're not back with that boyfriend, are you?"

"No. You don't need to worry about him."

"I heard you went to the movies with Dane Carmichael."

"Yes, I went to the movies with Dane." I didn't have to guess how she knew.

"He's a nice young man."

"He is."

"Dad said you promised to come back soon. Do you know when you'll be coming?"

"I've only just got back home." I didn't want to tell her my plans. Not yet. Not that I thought they'd change. I just didn't want her or anyone else organizing me. Lawrence had done enough of that for a lifetime.

"Okay. Well, let me know."

"I will. How's Dad today?"

"Not so good." She sounded a little downcast and my heart sagged.

"What's wrong?"

"Nothing definite. He just feels a bit off."

"I guess it's normal."

"I think so."

"I wish he'd— "

"Stop it, Kayla. He won't."

I let out a frustrated sigh. I still didn't understand why he wouldn't at least get a second opinion, but I had to let it go. "Okay. Sorry. And Mom…"

"Yes?"

"I love you."

Silence again. I hadn't told her that since I was a little girl. I'd shocked her.

"I... I love you too, sweetheart. I hope you're okay."

"I will be."

"I'm glad to hear that. Take care."

"I will. And give my love to Dad."

"I will."

After I ended the call, I made another coffee, grabbed a bagel and headed back to bed. I automatically flicked the television on, but even with so many channels, I failed to find anything that grabbed my interest. There were plenty of the reality type shows I often zoned out with, but I needed something more right now. I had a longing for something deeper, more meaningful.

I flicked the television off and picked up the Bible and continued reading where I'd left off last night. I surprised myself and read for more than an hour. I'd remembered what Dane had said, and asked God to help me understand it. The more I read, the more I wanted to read, but my heart moved inside me when I reached John chapter 3, verse 16. I'd heard this verse before but had never grasped its meaning. *For God so loved the world that He gave His one and only Son, that whoever believes in Him shall not perish but have eternal life.* This was what my dad believed. It was why he wasn't afraid of dying—he believed in eternal life. I let out a sigh and continued reading. I needed to know if Jesus really was the Son of God like this verse said He was, and could deliver the goods He promised to His believers.

I fell asleep again and woke as night was falling. Stepping out onto my balcony, I looked at the city and wondered what it was all about. So much activity, so much razzle-dazzle, but what purpose did it fulfill? I didn't think I wanted to play this game anymore. The peace and quiet of Shelton, and of one workshop in particular, held so much more appeal all of a sudden.

I'd rally myself and finish the tour, but after that, I'd seriously consider a change.

Skyping that night with Dane, I asked him if we could start doing a Bible study together. He almost fell off his stool, but he readily agreed. I told him the times would be irregular because of my schedule, but he didn't mind. He was just happy that I was searching.

22

DANE

DAWN. *"Surely there is a future, and your hope will not be cut off."*

I VISITED Ivan in the hospital every day. At first he said very little, and I was okay with that. I was there for him, a friend, and that was all that mattered. I was glad he knew that I'd been exactly where he was, feeling as if I couldn't live. Slowly he began to talk with me, and he allowed me to pray with him. He'd felt angry and frustrated that no one had noticed what had been happening in his home, not even his own mother. I told him that maybe she didn't know what to do, because I really believed she loved him. Sometimes it's hard to know what you'd do in a certain situation until you're in it yourself, so he shouldn't judge her. He didn't know what was going on in her life. Maybe she'd been scared of losing her husband if she confronted him with Ivan's accusations of abuse. Situations like that were complicated, and his mother was now suffering from guilt and was undergoing counseling to help her deal with it.

Ivan didn't want to press charges against his stepfather; he just wanted to forget it had ever happened. I didn't think this was right. The man had caused Ivan such distress that he wanted to take his life, but Ivan was adamant. He couldn't go back and live there, and he didn't want anything to do with him, but he also didn't want to go to court and testify. It was his word against his stepfather's. Who would the judge believe?

The family was in turmoil. How could Ivan's mother ever trust her husband again? He told her Ivan was lying. After talking with her son, she believed his story and told her husband he had to seek help or leave. He left. Now she was on her own with three children. It was so sad, but I knew that God would meet this family's needs. And maybe God would work in her husband's life and bring him back as a changed man. Time would tell.

Ivan returned to Boys' Club and visited my workshop as often as he could. During one of his visits, I asked him if he'd ever given his heart to the Lord. We'd spent many hours chatting about life in general but had skirted around the main issue. That afternoon I felt strongly he was ready, and so when I asked and he said no, he hadn't, I asked if he'd like to, and he said yes, he would. Leading him in a prayer of repentance and commitment was the most wonderful moment of my life. God's healing hand on Ivan's life was evident. His tears, genuine and real, glistened on his cheeks as I hugged him and welcomed him into God's family. I knew God would be gentle on him as he dealt with deep-seated issues in his life. God was like that. He knew exactly what we each needed and treated us accordingly. I felt privileged to be part of Ivan's life and have him consider me as his mentor.

I also felt privileged to be Kayla's mentor. The night she asked if we could study the Bible together, I felt all my prayers were being answered. She was searching, but she didn't accept everything blindly. In fact, she questioned just about everything. But she had an open heart and mind, and that was all she needed, because the answers were there, even if sometimes it took me a few days to find them.

We didn't discuss her plans for the future, although I got the impression that her heart was no longer in her music career. I figured she'd be back one day soon to visit her father and we could chat then. He was having his treatment and everyone seemed hopeful he would survive, but the times I'd been to visit he didn't look that great. He still wore his huge smile and talked about God's amazing love, which was a witness in itself, considering the discomfort he was in. His life was in God's hands; who was he to question his maker? I wasn't sure Kayla would accept this, but I prayed that one day soon she would.

23

KAYLA

SURRENDER. *"For by grace you have been saved through faith; and that not of yourselves, it is the gift of God; not as a result of works, so that no one may boast."*

I WANTED to get the tour over and done with, but I couldn't allow my change of heart to show, so I sat in the salon chair and chatted with my stylist as if nothing had happened.

"When did you change to brown? I don't remember you doing that."

"I did it myself. I took some time off and went home. Tried to stay under the radar."

"And did it work?"

"Not really."

"Now might be a good time for a change. How about we crop one side? A new hair style for your tour?"

I grimaced. If she'd suggested it a month ago, I might have agreed, but I didn't want to do that to my hair now.

"No. I'd prefer to keep it the same. Just a trim and redo the color."

"Okay. Whatever you want." She wasn't happy, but it was my hair.

Three hours later, Kayla Mac, with her trademark blue-black hair, was back. At least on the outside; on the inside, Kayla McCormack was undergoing a transformation.

I headed straight to rehearsal and threw myself into it as if it still meant the world to me. Lawrence was ecstatic with my enthusiasm and said I'd never sounded better. I'd decided that the only way to do this was to pretend nothing had changed. I owed my band and my fans that much. I'd give my all as I always did, and then I'd take a break. They didn't need to know I mightn't return.

After my time away, I was out of condition and struggled to make it through the entire rehearsal.

"You need to get to the gym," Lawrence said to me after we'd finished. He handed me a bottle of water and glared at me. "You've let yourself go."

I shrugged. "Sorry." I knew I had. I'd need to work hard to get my physical strength back in order to complete my tour.

"You've got three days."

"I'll go in the morning. "

"You need to go tonight." His expression showed no pity.

I groaned. I'd just done a three-hour rehearsal and my whole body ached. "Okay." I sighed and grabbed my gear.

By the time I arrived back at my apartment I was ready for bed. I grabbed a bottle of beer from the fridge and collapsed onto the sofa, and then I remembered my skype appointment with Dane. I was too tired to study the Bible, but I sure could do with seeing his face. He might be the one thing that would get me through the next month.

I picked up my laptop and called him. "Hey, nerd. How's your day been?"

"Good. I visited Ivan." The camera was all over the place as he moved to a stool, but I smiled at him anyway. Seeing his face and his workshop was like a balm for my sore body and soul.

"How is he?"

"All right, but it's going to take time. He's got a lot to deal with."

I smiled. "He's lucky to have you as a friend."

Dane steadied his screen. "Thank you. So, how was your day?"

"Long."

"I like your hair."

"Really?" I lifted my hand and touched it.

He chuckled. "No, not really."

"It's my stage hair."

"I can tell."

We chatted easily for the next hour. I didn't know where the time went, and even though I hadn't felt like doing a Bible study at the beginning, it was me who said we should. "Just a short one. Explain to me again how Jesus actually came to be. It's still difficult for me to accept what I was taught as a child."

As Dane patiently explained to me God's omnipotence, meaning that He's capable of doing anything He chooses, including coming to earth in human form and being born of a virgin, I began to see that my view of God was too limited, and by limiting Him, I was limiting my understanding. Dane told me that if I could accept that God was who He said He was, the

God of creation, almighty, all powerful and all knowing, then everything else would fall into place.

And thus began my crazy, weird month. Belting out songs on stage for fans who thought the sun shone from me. Hours spent at the gym maintaining my fitness so I could last the distance. Checking into and out of hotel after hotel. Keeping Lawrence happy by pretending this would last forever, and then skyping with Dane and talking about God, the best part of every day, before finally collapsing into my bed. I couldn't wait to call him and see his face. To hear about his day, what pots he was making, how Ivan was doing. Compared to my days, his were slow, quiet, peaceful. It was what I longed for. I was done with noise and busyness. Slowly, the month passed.

Lawrence tried to convince me not to end my career. I gave him a whole year's wage and told him to take a vacation before looking for another job. He said he didn't want another job; he'd wait for me to come back. I told him he might be waiting a long time.

I packed up my personal belongings, put my apartment up for rent, and booked a flight home.

THE CONGREGATION STARED at me as I walked in. My hair was still blue. I should have dyed it before I left, but I'd been so busy packing I'd forgotten about it until I was on the plane. I didn't care. I doubted Dane would care either.

I hadn't told him I was coming back; I wanted to surprise him, and what better way than to turn up at church? My parents would be even more surprised. My dad wasn't doing too well, and I couldn't wait to see him. I spied him and Mom sitting in a pew halfway down the church. I walked up behind them and placed a kiss on his cheek. His eyes lit up and he hugged me like the long-lost daughter that I was. My mom had tears in her eyes as she hugged me next. Dane just smiled from the pew in front and waited for me to finish the reunion with my folks. When I joined him, I slipped my hand into his and squeezed it. Finally I was home, and I'd never felt happier or more at peace.

But there was one more thing I needed to do. During the prayer time, I quietly invited Jesus into my life. I didn't want to cause a spectacle by walking to the front. I'd been on the front-line too long. Now it was time to take a back seat. I knew God wouldn't mind; He knew my heart. I was sorry for all the things I'd done wrong. I was His precious creation, lovingly made for His glory. He had a lot of work to do in my life, chipping off the rough edges, teaching me His ways, but I knew He'd forgiven me for all my wrong-doings. They were in the past; I had a clean slate. And I had the best mentor anyone could ask for. I wiped my eyes and smiled up at him. I didn't know what the future held for us, but I was so glad to have Dane as my best friend.

After the service ended, I shared with him that I'd left L.A. and walked away from my career, although I think he already knew.

"You've made my day." His eyes glistened as he smiled at me and gave me a big hug. He could barely speak.

"Thank you for being so patient."

"It's been a pleasure."

I smiled and told him I needed to share the news with my parents.

"Skype you later?"

I laughed. "How about a live chat?"

"Sounds great."

"I'll be back."

As I walked the short distance to reach my parents, people still stared at me even though they tried to pretend they weren't. Especially Mrs. Steward. I didn't care. If they couldn't look past my blue hair, that was their problem. When I reached my mom and dad, they asked me why I hadn't told them I was coming home. I said I wanted to surprise them. Then I said I had an even bigger surprise.

"What's that, sweetheart?" my dad asked. His face looked gaunt, but his eyes still twinkled when he squeezed my hand.

"What you've been praying for years for." My voice choked. I knew how much this would mean to them. I finally understood their love for God and their burning desire for me to know it too. "I asked Jesus into my life."

Once again, tears sprung from my mother's eyes and flowed down her cheeks. My father reached out and hugged me. "That's wonderful news. The best you could give us."

I nodded, unable to speak.

"Will you come home so we can catch up?"

I nodded again. "Do you mind if I invite Dane?"

My mother's eyes widened. "Of course not. Dane's always welcome."

I smiled. "I'll see you at home."

I returned to Dane and invited him to my parents' house for lunch. It wouldn't have been right not to go back with my parents, but the person I really wanted to be with was Dane. Inviting him for lunch was the perfect solution.

24

DANE

JOY. *"Take delight in the Lord, and he will give you the desires of your heart."*

SURREAL. That was the only word to describe sharing Sunday lunch with Kayla and her parents in their small but homey dining room after church that day. Kayla had given no indication she was returning to Shelton so soon, and now, having her so close that every time I looked up our gazes met, it filled me with great joy. But, if I were honest, this joy was also accompanied by a small amount of fear and trepidation over where this might lead. Was I ready for our relationship to extend beyond our special friendship? Is that what she wanted? *Is it what I wanted?*

I'd never allowed myself to consider that Kayla might look at me as more than a friend. But now, with her eyes brimming with tenderness and warmth, I dared to hope. Now she'd made her decision to follow Jesus, we had that common faith to connect us, but there was still so much to learn about each other. I was getting ahead of myself and was thankful when Stephen asked me about the Boys' Club. "I hear you're teaching them to make pots."

Although his cancer treatment had affected him physically, Stephen was still smiling, happy, and trusting God with the outcome of his illness. I could only hope that if ever I faced a situation like the one he was facing, I would do so with all the grace and courage he was showing. I wondered if God had used Stephen's illness to grab Kayla's attention. It certainly seemed so, although at first she'd blamed God for causing it. She was still struggling to understand why God allowed it to happen, but I prayed that with her newfound faith, she might come to see that what happens to us in life is less important than how we handle it, especially as this life is so temporal and short in the light of eternity. But Kayla was a baby Christian, just a few hours old, although we'd spent much time reading and discussing the Bible. She would grow in her faith and understanding, day by day, just as a baby grows and learns about the world. But I couldn't wait to see what God had planned for her; I was sure He'd use her voice and vitality for His Kingdom in some way.

But Kayla was distracting me again, and I hadn't answered her father. I turned my focus to him and laughed. "Yes, and it's been a real eye-opener. So much easier getting them to chat and share when they're up to their elbows in mud than plunked on bean bags listening to me drone on. And there's so many lessons to be drawn from the whole potting process. I don't know why I hadn't thought of it before."

"That's wonderful. God certainly knew what He was saying when He said to go down to the Potter's House."

I laughed again. "I'm not sure He actually meant my potter's house, but I'm happy the boys are enjoying it and learning a lot at the same time."

"And what about Ivan? How is he doing?"

"Great. In fact, out of all the boys, he's probably the most skilled. And he's much happier at home now. It's a pity his mother's struggling on her own, but the church ladies are supporting her, as you know." I smiled at Marianne. Despite caring for Stephen, she was often helping out with babysitting so Ivan's mom could go to work.

I caught Kayla's gaze and grinned. I couldn't help it. It was like a dream come true. And although I preferred her natural color, her blue hair was growing on me. As much as I enjoyed chatting with Kayla's parents, I couldn't wait to be alone with her. Finally, I asked if she'd like to see her pot. I'd finished it just yesterday, completely unaware that she'd be home today to see it in person. When I saw the bowl that I'd given her as a gift on her previous visit sitting on the kitchen counter, I smiled. I'd always wondered who she'd intended it for, and it warmed my heart to know it was her mother.

Kayla was eager to see her pot, and so after we helped clean the dishes, I thanked her parents for a lovely meal, and we left together in my pickup. I glanced at her to make sure I wasn't dreaming. I wasn't. She'd glanced at me at the same time, and as our gazes met, we shared a smile that warmed my heart. I reached out and squeezed her hand, something I would never have done before. "It's great to see you, Kayla."

"And it's great to see you too, Dane." Her smile widened and a sense of well-being flowed through me.

We drove the rest of the way in comfortable silence. I was glad, because I didn't know what else to say. I sensed this was the beginning of something new and wonderful, because every time my gaze met hers, my heart pounded a little faster. But we had to do this God's way; I wouldn't hurry it and run the risk of ruining what He'd done, and was doing, in both our lives. We were so different, but they say opposites attract. I was certainly attracted, and I hoped the feeling was mutual. I sensed it was.

When we arrived at my parents' home, my mom was outside in the garden and raised a brow when Kayla jumped down from the pickup. She knew that Kayla and I had become friends, and she'd voiced her concern once again that I'd get hurt. It might take time for her to accept that Kayla was a new person, but the change in her was already remarkable.

"Mom, you remember Kayla?" I gave her a warning look.

She let out a small laugh, set down her gardening tools, and stepped towards us. "Yes, I do. It's nice to see you, Kayla. I think I saw you in church this morning."

I laughed. Of course Mom would have seen her. No one could have missed her.

Kayla smiled and took my Mom's extended hand. "Yes, I was there. Nice to meet you properly, Mrs. Carmichael."

My mom gave a dismissive wave. "Oh, please. Call me Marjorie. Mrs. Carmichael makes me sound so old. Are you here to see your father?"

"Kind of. I've taken an indefinite break, so I might be hanging around a while."

A momentary look of alarm crossed Mom's face.

I understood how she felt, but everyone deserved a second chance. I knew she considered Kayla to be damaged goods, but God had wiped her slate clean. My mom was yet to know that. I placed my hand gently on her shoulder. "Why don't you make us some coffee and we can have a chat after I show Kayla her finished pot?"

She looked less than happy but agreed anyway.

"We won't be long." I directed Kayla around the side and into my workshop.

"I don't think your mom likes me. I guess I don't blame her," she said once we were inside.

I sensed the hurt in her voice and I had a sudden urge to comfort her. I stepped towards her, placed my hands on her shoulders, and gazed into her eyes. "God has forgiven you for everything and He's given you a new start. My mom doesn't know that yet, but I'd like to tell her and my dad, if that's okay?"

When she nodded, a lone tear rolled slowly down her cheek. I gathered her into my arms and held her. "I've wanted to do this for so long. I never thought it would happen." I rested my cheek against her head and thanked God for bringing Kayla home.

25

KAYLA

ASSURANCE. *"Weeping may tarry for the night, But joy cometh in the morning."*

"IT'S SO BEAUTIFUL. You've done such a great job." I inspected my pot that Dane had completed, marveling not only at its smoothness and perfect shape, but at the lovely artwork. "How did you know strawberries were my favorite?"

A coy grin grew on his face. "Your father told me."

"He didn't!"

"He did. When I visited him recently, he told me about the secret late night ice cream dates the two of you used to have."

I shook my head as I ran my hand over the smooth surface and wondered how long it had taken him. Each strawberry was slightly different from each of the others, and the detail astounded me. "Well, it's beautiful." I lifted my face and smiled into his eyes. "Thank you. It's amazing to think it was just a lump of dirt when I started it."

"I could preach a sermon on that."

I laughed. "I know you could. Maybe we can skype tonight and you can preach it to me then."

He slipped his arms around me and looked deep into my eyes. "How about I give it to you in person?"

"Okay." I stretched up and popped a kiss on his cheek. "That's a deal. But first, we need to get that coffee."

His shoulders sagged. "You're right. Come on, let's go."

I carefully placed the pot into its box and took Dane's hand. It was strange. Neither of us had said anything about how our relationship had changed, but it had, and it felt right. I longed to be close to him, but I knew he'd want to do it God's way, which would be difficult for me, as I'd had a habit of not doing things God's way up until now. I had a lot to learn, but I was much like that pot; if Dane could create something beautiful from a lump of dirt, I knew God could make something even more beautiful out of my life. He might need to weed out the stones and prickles and pull and knead and pummel me to get me into shape, but I knew enough to understand that He'd do this because He loved me. I didn't need to hear Dane's sermon, but I'd listen anyway. In fact, I could listen to him explain the things of God forever. But now, we needed to chat with his parents. I hoped when his mom heard my story, she'd see me with fresh eyes, as a child of God, a sinner saved by grace, cleansed by the blood of Jesus.

Dane's parents were polite but cautious, which was to be expected. We sat in their living room, drinking coffee and eating the best chocolate brownies I've ever tasted, but we skirted around the main topic of conversation. Their suspicious eyes told me they didn't trust me. Like all the townsfolk, they were aware of my scandalous relationship with Gregor

Dubois, and possibly some, if not all, of the failed relationships before him. My track record wasn't great. Then there was my music. I knew they considered it evil, just like my mother did. They were conservative Christian people, so I guess I couldn't blame them. My songs *were* out there. They also would have been aware of my poor lifestyle choices—my drinking in particular. They didn't know that I hadn't had a drink in a month. Not since the night I started doing Bible studies via skype with their son.

After we'd exhausted all the small talk, Dane cleared his throat and reached for my hand. His mom's eyes widened. I stiffened. I'd never been in such a situation before. Dane ran his thumb gently over the top of my hand, giving me assurance that he would take control and not leave me to flounder. I so appreciated this about him. Yes, he was quiet, but he was also solid and trustworthy. Something Gregor Dubois definitely was not.

"Mom, Dad, I know you're concerned, but Kayla made a momentous decision this morning in church." He paused and gave me a smile full of encouragement and love before turning back to them. "You might be surprised to know that we've been doing Bible studies together for the past month."

His mom's forehead creased. "But how?"

"Via skype. Even when Kayla was exhausted after a concert, she'd call me so we could do a short study. She never missed, and this morning, she gave her life to the Lord."

I swallowed hard and pushed back tears. Not that long ago I wasn't even sure that God existed, yet He'd reached out to me and opened the eyes of my heart and soul. Now I now had a deep assurance that He not only existed, but that He was a loving Father who cared deeply for me. I felt quite overcome with the change that had occurred in me.

Dane's parents look stunned. They blinked; they looked at him and then at me, and then they smiled. It was his mom who spoke first. "I don't know what to say, other than you've taken us by surprise. We never expected this, but of course we're pleased. To hear that anyone has given their life to the Lord is cause for celebration."

I returned her smile and said that I understood.

"Kayla and I have become good friends," Dane said.

His dad shifted his gaze between us. "You don't say?"

"I'd like you to accept her, blue hair and all. I think she might be hanging around here quite often." Dane looked at me and winked.

I stifled a chuckle and then spoke to his parents. "Don't worry. I'll be visiting the salon tomorrow."

"I wouldn't be in too much of a hurry. I quite like it." A lopsided grin grew on his dad's face as he took another brownie from the plate and took a bite.

"It's been growing on me, too." Dane laughed and squeezed my hand.

"Maybe I'll leave it blue then." I joined in the laughter, pleased that the tension in the room had diffused.

Dane and I stayed only a short while longer and then we excused ourselves. Once outside, despite the chill of late afternoon, he took my hand and led me into the backyard and through an old wrought iron gate I'd not noticed before. "I want to show you something."

I walked slowly to match his pace. He never complained about his leg, in fact, he said it reminded him to focus on God and not himself. I didn't understand that, but I guessed I might one day. Gregor Dubois would laugh if he saw me now, but the last I'd heard, his wife had told him to leave, so who had the last laugh now? Certainly not me. It was strange how things could turn around so quickly, but I wouldn't have it any other way. "What do you want to show me?"

Dane stopped and faced me, his warm hazel eyes brimming with tenderness as he searched my face. Around us, knee-high grass rustled gently in the light breeze. "Nothing. I just wanted to be alone with you."

I exhaled a long sigh of contentment and an indefinable sense of rightness flowed through me.

He lifted his hand and fingered a loose strand of hair on my cheek. "I've always loved you, Kayla. It might have started with a childhood crush, but God has brought us together, and the more I've come to know you, the more I've come to love you." He paused and swallowed hard. I could sense he was nervous and my heart went out to him. He was so sweet.

He took a deep breath. "I guess what I'm trying to say is, will you be my girl?"

I threw my arms around his neck and kissed his cheek. "Of course I will!"

He let out a relieved sigh and looked deeply into my eyes. "I'll never hurt you, Kayla."

"And I'll never hurt you, Dane. You can be sure of that."

We shared a smile full of the promise of wonderful things to come. I longed for him to kiss me, but that would have to wait. We needed to do things God's way.

26

DANE

COMMITMENT. *"I found the one my heart loves."*

IN THE FOUR months Kayla and I had been dating, our relationship had grown stronger by the day, as had her faith in God. We still had our regular Bible studies, just not over skype. We now held them in my workshop, and we often shared them with the boys from church after their pottery class.

Kayla had also struck up a close friendship with Ivan, which warmed my heart no end. She'd started writing songs of life and love, of hope, redemption and second chances, and Ivan often played along with her on his guitar. On several occasions, they'd played these songs in church. She was working on a new album under the name of "Kayla". A new identity. A new life. A new song. God was so good.

I wanted to ask her to marry me. I loved her, and never wanted to be without her, but what if she said no? Niggling doubt stopped me from asking, but one afternoon after the boys had left and we were alone in my workshop, I decided to face my doubt head-on.

My heart pounded as I stepped closer to her. She was working on a new song. I was hesitant to interrupt, but I couldn't put it off any longer. "I made a special pot for you."

She looked up, angling her head. "What for?"

"Come and see."

"Now?"

I nodded.

She placed her guitar in its stand and took my hand. "This sounds mysterious."

I sat her in my best chair and although I knew my leg would hurt, I kneeled in front of her. I'd been thinking of doing something more romantic, but the moment had arrived before any plans had developed. I figured that the place and situation were of less importance than the actual question itself.

I took her hand and looked deep into her wide eyes. Love for her coursed through my veins. I smiled and swallowed hard. "I want to spend the rest of my life with you, Kayla. I love you deeply, and my life is so much better with you in it. Never in my wildest dreams had I thought you might love me too, especially when you couldn't even remember me, but I thank God that He brought you back into my life, and I'm hoping with everything that is within me that you'll agree to be my wife."

Tears welled in her eyes. Our gazes were locked for what seemed minutes, but in reality was just a moment. Her face broke into a beautiful, warm smile and she threw her arms around my neck. "Yes, Dane. I would love to be your wife."

Joy surged through me like hot chocolate on a cold,

winter's night, followed by relief. I should never have doubted. I held her tight and planted kisses all though her hair, which was no longer blue, but brown, smooth and smelled fresh like the flowers in my mother's garden.

She drew back and gazed into my eyes and smiled. "So, where's the pot?"

I laughed. Of course, the pot. I'd almost forgotten. I selected the tiniest pot I'd ever made from the shelf to my right and handed it to my bride-to-be, holding my breath as she carefully raised the lid.

I'd never bought a ring before, and I hoped she'd like it. It was simple, and perhaps not what she might have chosen.

I let my breath out when she looked up, her face beaming. "Dane, it's beautiful!"

I smiled. "Can I?"

She nodded and handed me the pot. I carefully lifted the simple, white-gold solitaire diamond ring out of its earthen container and slipped it slowly onto her finger. "Kayla, I want to spend the rest of my life with you, and this is my promise to love and cherish you with all my heart."

Tears flowed down her cheeks as she helped me stand. I bit back a grimace as pain stabbed my leg, but with Kayla's arms around me, and a whole new life to look forward to, I quickly forgot all about any pain.

27

KAYLA

BITTERSWEET. *"My grace is sufficient for you, for my power is made perfect in weakness."*

OUR ENGAGEMENT WAS SHORT; my father was dying. The treatment hadn't been successful and the cancer had spread. I finally understood that sometimes we have to accept what is and believe that God knows what's best. My dad would be going Home soon, as he continued to call it, but before he did, I wanted to walk down the aisle on his arm.

The night before my wedding, I joined him in the kitchen for possibly our last late-night ice cream date. He was so thin and gaunt, but he still smiled when I entered.

"Excited?" he asked as I grabbed a bowl and scooped strawberry ice cream into it.

I nodded. "I can't wait."

"I'm so happy for you, sweetheart. Dane's a good man."

"The best."

"He told me a long time ago he was going to marry you."

I laughed in surprise. "He did? When?"

"When he was in the third or fourth grade. He asked if he could marry you if he was a really good boy and kept his grades up. And he said he'd pray really hard until God answered his prayers."

I laughed until tears pricked my eyes. "I didn't even remember him from school, but God answered his prayers, anyway."

"As He did mine." My dad smiled wistfully as he squeezed my hand. "Not that Dane would marry you, but that you'd find inner peace. And that I'd see you truly happy before I passed on."

"Oh, Dad. I don't know that I can bear it." I brushed tears off my cheek.

"God will never give you more than you can bear, sweetheart. He'll give you strength you never knew you had."

"You're so brave."

"No, I just know that God loves me and has prepared a home for me in heaven, and that I'll see all of my family again one day. It won't be a goodbye forever; it will just be a goodbye for now. But anyway, it's your special day tomorrow. Let's not think on these things right now. Let's eat ice cream."

I blew out a breath and smiled, and then ate ice cream. What else could I do?

THE FOLLOWING MORNING, my mother came to my room and helped me prepare for the most precious day of my life. The rift between us had healed; she'd apologized for being so judgmental, and I'd told her I didn't blame her. I knew the heartache my poor lifestyle choices had caused her, and I felt bad.

My sister Jennifer arrived as I stepped out of the shower. The rift between the two of us was also healing but still had a way to go. She didn't believe the change in me was permanent and was waiting for me to revert to my old ways. Words wouldn't convince her, only my changed attitudes and life choices would do that, but for now at least, she was happy to be my matron of honor.

I was yet to make any close friends in Shelton. Most folks held the same opinion of me as Jennifer, but it didn't concern me; I was about to marry my best friend.

A little later, wearing the soft organza drop waisted wedding dress my mom had made for me, I linked my arm through my dad's and smiled at him before we began the slow walk down the aisle towards my beloved.

28

DANE

LOVE. "And now these three remain: faith, hope and love. But the greatest of these is love."

I COULD BARELY BREATHE as she walked towards me. Never had I seen her more beautiful; I was truly a blessed man. It took forever for Kayla to reach me; I clenched and unclenched my hands many times as she approached slowly on her father's arm, but our gazes, fixed on each other's, never wavered.

I smiled at Stephen as he finally placed her hand in mine. I knew in my heart that this gesture was more than a physical one. He only had a short time left on this earth, and he was entrusting his precious daughter to my care. It was such a responsibility, but also such a privilege, and one that I would not take lightly.

I squeezed her hand and smiled, and then we turned to face Reverend Matthew.

"We're gathered here today in the sight of God and the

presence of friends and loved ones to witness the union of Dane and Kayla. Marriage is the oldest and most sacred of all social institutions, ordained by God Himself."

I tried to focus on his words, which I knew were important. The commitment we were about to make was serious and sacred. He prayed over us and read some passages from the Bible, starting with 1 John 3, verse 18. "Dear children, let us not love with words or speech but with actions and in truth."

We both knew that love was more than words which could be said so lightly but then forgotten, but it was good to be reminded of this. We'd written our own vows, and as we faced each other, I looked deeply into Kayla's eyes and promised to love and cherish her for the rest of my life. "I can't wait to wake up beside you every morning. To put a smile on your face and to treat you as my princess. To grow in our faith together, and to face whatever life holds for us together, and with God."

Kayla brushed a tear from her eye as she too promised to love and cherish me for the rest of her days. Words I'd always wanted to hear but had never in my wildest dreams expected to.

I couldn't ask for anything more. Except to be declared husband and wife. Our eyes were locked together as Reverend Matthew spoke those wonderful words.

"Dane and Kayla, through their words today, have joined together in holy matrimony. They have exchanged their vows before God and these witnesses, and have pledged their commitment to each other, and have declared the same by the joining of hands and the exchange of rings. I now pronounce them husband and wife. Those whom God hath joined together, let no one put asunder." He turned and looked at me, a playful grin on his face. "Dane, you may now kiss your bride."

I rubbed my hands together and winked at my wife. Kayla knew how long I'd waited for this moment. I gathered her into my arms and placed my mouth gently over hers, devouring her softness. Our kiss was warm, sweet and perfect; it was everything I'd hoped it would be and so much more.

Everyone cheered and clapped when Reverend Matthew introduced us as Mr. And Mrs. Carmichael. I kept her close as we hugged and kissed our parents in turn, and then the rest of our families and friends.

Our wedding breakfast was simple; neither of us wanted anything elaborate. We'd chosen to live a simple life and hoped that one day God would bless us with children to share it with, but in the meantime, I would continue making pots and mentoring the church boys, and Kayla would write songs that spoke of love, hope, redemption and second chances.

Her father went home three weeks later, surrounded by his loving family. His last words to us were to put our trust in God, and to keep the greatest commandment of all; to love Him with all our hearts and with all our souls and with all our minds, and to love our neighbors as ourselves.

I hugged Kayla and comforted her. We knew we'd see her father again one day in glory, but our loss here and now would be real and tangible; he would no longer be here with us in Shelton. Our children would never know him, and Kayla would never have another late-night ice cream date with him. But his sickness had brought us together, and for that we were eternally grateful. We would have preferred him to live, but in his death, he brought glory to God by the way he loved and trusted right to the very end. His life spurred us on to live a life worthy of our calling, which we intended to do to the best of our abilities.

NOTE FROM THE AUTHOR

I hope you enjoyed *The Homecoming*, and that it encouraged you in your own personal walk with the Lord. You'll find further inspiration and encouragement on The Potter's House Books Website, and by reading the other books in the series. Read them all and be encouraged and uplifted!

Find all the books on Amazon and on The Potter's House Books website:

- Book 1: The Homecoming, by Juliette Duncan
- Book 2: When it Rains, by T.K. Chapin
- Book 3: Heart Unbroken, by Alexa Verde (pre-order March 27, 2018)
- Book 4: Long Way Home, by Brenda S Anderson (pre-order April 10, 2018)
- Book 5: Promises Renewed, By Mary Manners (pre-order April 24, 2018)
- Book 6: A Vow Redeemed, by Kristen M. Fraser (pre-order May 8, 2018)
- Book 7: Restoring Faith, by Marion Ueckermann (pre-order May 22, 2018)
- Book 8: Unchained, by Juliette Duncan (pre-order June 12, 2018)
- Book 9 – 21 to be advised

Be notified of all new releases by joining Juliette's Readers' list. (www.julietteduncan.com/subscribe). You will also receive a free copy of *"Hank and Sarah - A Love Story"*, *a clean love story with God at the center.*

Enjoyed *The Homecoming?* You can make a big difference... Help other people find this book by writing a review and telling them why you liked it. Honest reviews of my books help bring them to the attention of other readers just like yourself, and I'd be very grateful if you could spare just five minutes to leave a review (it can be as short as you like) on the book's Amazon page.

Blessings,

Juliette

OTHER POTTER'S HOUSE BOOKS

Find all of the Potter's House Books at:

http://pottershousebooks.com/our-books/

OTHER BOOKS BY JULIETTE DUNCAN

Find all of Juliette Duncan's books on her website:
www.julietteduncan.com/library

THE TRUE LOVE SERIES

Immerse yourself into the lives of Ben, Tessa and Jayden...

After her long-term relationship falls apart, Tessa Scott is left questioning God's plan for her life, and is feeling vulnerable and unsure of how to move forward. Ben Williams is struggling to keep the pieces of his life together after his wife of fourteen years walks out on him and their teenage son.

Stephanie, Tessa's housemate, knows the pain both Tessa and Ben have suffered. When she inadvertently sets up a meeting between them, there's no denying that they are drawn to each other, but will that mutual attraction do more harm than good?

Can Tessa and Ben let go of their leftover baggage and examine their feelings in order to follow a new path? Are they prepared for the road ahead, regardless of the challenges? Will they trust God to equip them with all they need for the journey ahead?

"Since reading the Shadows Series, I've been hooked on Juliette Duncan's writing. Tender Love is another example of her talent for bringing characters to life and weaving a story with all the elements of superior storytelling. Totally clean, yet written with adult situations; the pain of breakups, broken marriages, rearing teenagers, job challenges, maintaining relationships with parents and friends. And in the center of the story, we find two people who, while recuperating from painful situations in their personal lives, find hope and love, looking forward into their future together. The scriptures and Biblical principles are so masterfully worked into the book, they complement the story, rather than pull us away, as some, less talented writers sometimes do. This is not a long read, but one which will satisfy." Amazon Customer

---

The Precious Love Series

Best read after "The True Love Series" but can be read separately

Book 1 - Forever Cherished

Now Tessa's dream of living in the country has been realized, she wants to share her and Ben's blessings with others, but when a sad, lonely woman comes to stay, Tessa starts to think she's bitten off more than she can chew, and has to rely on her faith at every turn.

Leah Maloney is carrying a truck-load of disappointments from the past and has almost given up on life. Her older sister arranges for her to spend time at 'Misty Morn', but Leah is suspicious of her sister's motives.

"Forever Cherished" is a stand-alone novel, but is better read as a follow-on from "The True Love Series" books.

Book 2 - Forever Faithful

Although half a world separates them, Jayden Williams has never stopped loving Angela Morgan, the green-eyed, red haired girl who captured his heart and led him to the Lord in the hills of Montana several years earlier.

When he becomes the victim of a one-punch attack and is lying unconscious in a hospital bed half-way around the world, Angela knows she has no choice but to go to him. What if he died and she wasn't there for him? She'd never forgive herself.

But Angela has a boyfriend who isn't happy about her friendship with Jayden. When her boyfriend arrives on Jayden's grandparents' doorstep unannounced, Angela has to decide if her friendship with Jayden is stronger than her love for Cole. Can she leave Jayden like Cole wants her to and risk losing his love?

Will God answer her prayers and restore Jayden to health, or will she need to accept the outcome as God's will, whether he lives or dies?

Book 3 - Forever His

Coming Soon!

———

The Shadows Series

An inspirational romance, a story of passion and love, and of God's inexplicable desire to free people from pasts that haunt them so they can live a life full of His peace, love and forgiveness, regardless of the circumstances. *"Lingering Shadows"* is set in England, and follows the story of Lizzy, a headstrong, impulsive young lady from a privileged background, and Daniel, a roguish Irishman who sweeps her off her feet. But can Lizzy leave the shadows of her past behind and give Daniel the love he deserves, and will Daniel find freedom and release in God?

Praise for "The Shadows Series"

"I absolutely LOVE this series. I grew to connect with each of the characters with each passing page. If you are looking for a story with real-life situations & great character development, with the love of God interwoven throughout the pages, I HIGHLY recommend The Shadows Series Box Set by Juliette Duncan!" JLB

"Amazing story, one of the best I have ever read. Gives us so much information regarding alcoholism and abusive behavior. It also gives us understanding on how to respond. The Bible was well presented to assist with understanding how to accomplish the behaviors necessary to deal with the situations." Jeane M

The Madeleine Richards Series

Although the 3 book series is intended mainly for pre-teen/Middle Grade girls, it's been read and enjoyed by people of all ages.

Hank and Sarah - A Love Story

The Prequel to "The Madeleine Richards Series" is a FREE thank you gift for joining my mailing list. www.julietteduncan.com/subscribe

ABOUT THE AUTHOR

Juliette Duncan is passionate about writing true to life Christian romances that will touch her readers' hearts and make a difference in their lives. Drawing on her own often challenging real-life experiences, Juliette writes deeply emotional stories that highlight God's amazing love and faithfulness, for which she's eternally grateful. Juliette lives in Brisbane, Australia. She and her husband have five adult children and seven grandchildren whom they love dearly, as well as an elderly long-haired dachshund and a little black cat. When not writing, Juliette and her husband love exploring the great outdoors.

Connect with Juliette:
Email: author@julietteduncan.com
Website: www.julietteduncan.com
Facebook: www.facebook.com/JulietteDuncanAuthor
BookBub: www.bookbub.com/authors/juliette-duncan

Made in the USA
Las Vegas, NV
10 September 2021